DIRTY DEALING

Toylike though his small sawed-off might be, when he slammed the butt of it into Fargo's midsection, Fargo did exactly what Bradshaw wanted him to do—folded in half and fought a strong desire to vomit.

Not that Bradshaw stopped there. Men like him never did. He was staking out his territory—the entire town of Cumberland, in his case—the way a predatory animal does, and he obviously wanted Fargo to understand that he was in change.

He cracked Fargo on the side of the head.

"Now we understand each other, Mister Fargo."

The boot came swift and sure out of nowhere, catching Fargo just below the ribs. This time, he couldn't take it anymore. He sprang from his kneeling position, hurled himself upon the bigger man and drove him all the way back to the wall.

Fargo smashed three savage fists into Bradshaw's midsection. It was now the lawman's turn to fold in half. But Fargo wasn't done. . . .

THE
TRAILSMAN
#253

DEAD
MAN'S HAND

by

Jon Sharpe

A SIGNET BOOK

SIGNET
Published by New American Library, a division of
Penguin Putnam Inc., 375 Hudson Street,
New York, New York 10014, U.S.A.
Penguin Books Ltd, 80 Strand,
London WC2R 0RL, England
Penguin Books Australia Ltd, Ringwood,
Victoria, Australia
Penguin Books Canada Ltd, 10 Alcorn Avenue,
Toronto, Ontario, Canada M4V 3B2
Penguin Books (N.Z.) Ltd, 182–190 Wairau Road,
Auckland 10, New Zealand

Penguin Books Ltd, Registered Offices:
Harmondsworth, Middlesex, England

First published by Signet, an imprint of New American Library,
a division of Penguin Putnam Inc.

First Printing, November 2002
10 9 8 7 6 5 4 3 2 1

The first chapter of this book previously appeared in *Kansas City Swindle,*
the two hundred fifty-second volume in this series.

 REGISTERED TRADEMARK—MARCA REGISTRADA

Printed in the United States of America

PUBLISHER'S NOTE
This is a work of fiction. Names, characters, places, and incidents either
are the product of the author's imagination or are used fictitiously,
and any resemblance to actual persons, living or dead, events, or locales
is entirely coincidental.

BOOKS ARE AVAILABLE AT QUANTITY DISCOUNTS WHEN USED TO PROMOTE
PRODUCTS OR SERVICES. FOR INFORMATION PLEASE WRITE TO PREMIUM
MARKETING DIVISION, PENGUIN PUTNAM INC., 375 HUDSON STREET, NEW
YORK, NEW YORK 10014.

The Trailsman

Beginnings . . . they bend the tree and they mark the man. Skye Fargo was born when he was eighteen. Terror was his midwife, vengeance his first cry. Killing spawned Skye Fargo, ruthless, cold-blooded murder. Out of the acrid smoke of gunpowder still hanging in the air, he rose, cried out a promise never forgotten.

The Trailsman they began to call him all across the West: searcher, scout, hunter, the man who could see where others only looked, his skills for hire but not his soul, the man who lived each day to the fullest, yet trailed each tomorrow. Skye Fargo, the Trailsman, the seeker who could take the wildness of a land and the wanting of a woman and make them his own.

Oregon Territory, 1861—
In some casinos you lose not
only your money but your life—something
the Trailsman aims to put a stop to.

1

Skye Fargo was not surprised to hear gunfire. He was
well aware of Cumberland, Oregon's, reputation as a
hell town and haven for gamblers, gunnies, and ladies
of the night.

As the tall, black-haired man with the lake-blue eyes
guided his Ovaro stallion through the chill rain and
toward the lights of town, he realized that he was glad
he'd be sleeping in a warm, dry bed tonight. He'd been
six days traveling through the splendor of this territory
that included the rugged sight of the mountains, which
the glaciers had carved into breathtaking peaks, gorges,
and ravines. As he drove deeper toward the plateau,
timberlands as dense as he'd ever seen appeared. Black
walnut, Ponderosa pine, and Sitka spruce sprawled over
the foothills.

The farmlands he eventually came to showed why so
many hundreds of covered wagons had stopped when
they reached the Willamette Valley here. It offered some
of the most fertile lands in the entire west. The trail
grew melancholy only as he neared the Indian reserva-
tion, where so many braves had been slaughtered at the
behest of a mentally unbalanced Indian agent. Many different tribes now sang of the slaughter. The tragedy was
one of legend among Indians of all tribes.

Cumberland, whose WELCOME sign boasted 7,423
souls, was the expected mixture of false fronts and one-
story buildings. As his pinto sluiced through the muddy
main street, Fargo noted that the buildings were well
kept and that the board sidewalks on both sides of the

street looked new. The telegraph office was open late as was the general store. Sure signs of prosperity.

Say what you might about betting parlors being havens for gamblers, they brought a lot of revenue into a town; revenue that benefited most of its citizens to some degree. But along with gambling came cardsharps, bunco artists of all stripes, and hoodlums.

Fargo found a livery where a middle-aged black man named James took one look at Fargo's horse and said, "Now that's a beautiful specimen."

"Thank you," Fargo replied.

"Yessir, I see just about every kind of equine there is. But I sure don't see one like this very often. I don't suppose he's for sale?"

"Afraid not."

"I got a standing order from Mister Clymer—gentleman who owns this livery—that if I ever see an outstanding piece of horseflesh, I'm to tell him right away. And this one here sure qualifies as an outstanding piece of horseflesh." He wore an old sweater, flannel shirt, work trousers. He talked around a corn cob pipe tucked deep into the corner of his mouth. His face and his voice conveyed a thoughtful intelligence.

"Well, I sure can't imagine selling him," Fargo said. "Not after all the things we've been through together."

Then he went looking for a hotel so he could take care of himself for the night.

He was surprised to find that two of the casinos were dark, their front doors padlocked. He was also surprised to see four elderly people wearing Amish-style hats parading in front of the Ruby Rooster, the only casino that was still open. They were chanting in some kind of protest.

> "Gambling is a sin . . .
> Satan works here . . .
> Gambling is shameful . . .
> The devil's den . . ."

The people leaving and entering the casino didn't pay any attention to the protesters. Apparently, this was a regular occurrence, the placard-carrying people paying the casino a nightly visit.

Fargo went on to the nearest hotel. It wasn't fancy, but it looked clean and felt warm. So he walked up to the desk and got himself a room for the night.

The beefy clerk with the boozy nose sneezed, sliding a finger beneath his nose as he did so. The finger turned suddenly green. He looked at the green stuff, and Fargo looked at the green stuff. Then the clerk wiped his finger off on his trouser leg and smiled as if nothing at all had happened. "Guess you'll be wanting a room," he said.

"Guess so," Fargo replied.

"Well, Lord knows there's nothing better than a dry bed on a wet and cold night."

"Yeah," Fargo said. "I noticed that two of the casinos are closed. What happened?"

"Oh, it's a long story." The clerk obviously didn't want to talk about it.

"Those protesters have anything to do with it?"

He shrugged. "Sort of."

"Somebody should shoot those bastards," a man in a derby said from an armchair where he was reading the newspaper. "I used to come to Cumberland to have myself some fun. Me and a lot of other drummers. Now the only casino left is the Ruby Rooster. I don't know how much longer it can hold out, either."

"What's going on here?" Fargo said.

The derby man said, "Like Earl here says, it's a long story, mister."

Fargo hefted his saddlebags. "My room ready?"

"Should just about be," Earl said. "I got Doris the maid up there now. We're full up. We don't usually rent out that room. That's the way Doris wants it."

"I suppose if I ask you why you don't rent it out you'll tell me it's a—"

"—long story."

Instead of being sinister, the reluctance to talk was actually funny. Fargo expected hotel people to be talkers. That's what people did in hotels. Talked. Drank a little, sure. Had some sex if they were lucky enough, sure. But mostly they talked. Especially desk clerks and drummers. But Fargo got the sense that these two had talked so much about the subject that they were tired of it. It was just too damned boring to walk back through again.

Fargo headed upstairs.

The carpeting in the hallway was clean. The sconces were covered for safety. Somebody had sprinkled some nice-smelling stuff all over the walls. This was a good place to stay.

When he opened the door to Room 107, he saw a small but supremely well-fashioned blonde girl using a feather duster on the top of a bureau. She was singing to herself in a sweet, slightly off-key feminine voice, a sentimental mountain song, and apparently didn't hear him open the door. So he stood for a moment enjoying the view, the nicely rounded curve of buttock outlined against the dungaree bottom and the thrust of breast against the white cotton blouse.

When she became aware of him she smiled and said, "You're a big one." She didn't look startled at all. She had a country girl kind of composure he liked right away.

"You should see my horse," Fargo said, coming into the room. "I mean, if you think I'm big."

He dropped his saddlebags on the floor and walked over to the window. There was a shadowy alley below, and a fog was settling on the rooftops of small houses in the distance.

"There you go," the girl said, using the duster one last time. "I put it all back together again."

"The clerk downstairs said there was something special about this room. And now you say that you put it all back together again. Something happened here?"

She shrugged. She had one of those sweet small-town faces that just made you feel good to look at. "Well, it's kind of—"

He laughed and stuck out a halting hand. "Don't say it."

"Don't say what?"

"That it's a long story."

"Well, actually, it kind of is."

"Well, I've got plenty of time on my hands, so let me

4

hear it. And then let me ask you a couple of other questions, too . . . Any beer in this hotel?"

"There's a saloon downstairs."

"Good. Why don't you go get us some beer, and then you can tell me all about this room and this town. Say— are you old enough to drink beer?"

"I sure am. And I drink beer all the time, for your information. I'm nineteen."

"My name's Skye Fargo."

"Mine's Doris Mallory."

"Well, Doris Mallory, you go get us some beer and then you come back here and we'll talk. How about that?"

She smiled. There was just the slightest hint of sexuality in her expression. "You sure are a big one. And that's how I like 'em, I guess." The smile was wider now. "Big."

"Nobody was sure where Suzanna came from," Doris told Skye over a bucket of beer twenty minutes later. "Just showed up one day along about four months ago. Everybody fell in love with her. She was one of the most beautiful girls I ever saw. She worked over at the Ruby Rooster and had this room right here in the hotel. She was a dance girl but never a prostitute. She got to be as big a draw at the casino as the gambling."

"And what happened to her?"

"Killed herself. Right here in this room. I was the one who found her."

"You sure she killed herself?"

"Well, Skye, it sure looked that way. She had the gun next to her head. The wound was right above her temple."

"Why would a beautiful young girl kill herself?"

"I don't know," Doris said, tears gleaming in her eyes. "And it was kinda selfish of her is the way I feel. She always said I was the best friend she had in the whole world. I helped her do a lot of things—helped her get a horse, took her over to the bank and introduced her to Neil Anderson so she could open up her safety box, even tried to fix her up with some of the more respectable men around here."

"Did she go out with any of them?"

"No. That was the funny thing about her. You'd expect her to really enjoy herself, the way she looked and all. But she didn't. She didn't laugh much, for one thing. She was always real intense, like she had somethin' on her mind she wasn't lettin' you know about."

"So you didn't have any hint that she was going to kill herself?"

"Not at all. I know it's selfish—but the least she could've done was leave me a note."

She began sobbing so violently she almost knocked her beer glass off the small table between the chairs they were sitting on. Fargo went over and brought her to her feet, took her in his arms, and pressed her head against his wide chest. He began to stroke the fine silk of her blonde hair. And as he did so, he felt both of them begin to stir to a desire that they'd both been aware of since he'd first walked into this room.

She filled his mouth with her hot, hungry tongue, guiding his hand down to the fullness of her breast. Her nipple already poked hard at the material of her blouse and it was only moments later that he began freeing her of her clothing altogether. Her breasts spilled free, bouncing for a moment. He put his tongue on one of her nipples and she cried out as if she'd been stabbed. Some women had extremely sensitive breasts, and she was one of those women.

She returned the favor by liberating his manly steed, stroking the considerable length of it, touching it as if she could not quite believe the size of the treasure she had unearthed.

She gasped, "I want it in me now, Skye. All of it. Please."

They did a comic little dance over to the bed, moving in mincing steps because their pants were down around their ankles. Moments after reaching the bed, they were naked. Skye wanted to pleasure her completely, so before entering her he eased her legs apart and began to explore the rich, dark, sweet-smelling cave of her womanhood.

He moved his tongue expertly, quickly at some times, slowly at others, always seeking those places that evoked her startled cries of ecstacy. When his tongue began flicking maniacally she began to buck and grind as if she was riding a bronco and holding on for dear life. He kept this up until she did the impossible—used her slight hundred-pound frame to drag him up to her and guide his manhood inside her.

Her previous bucking and grinding was nothing compared to what came next. Nails raked his shoulders and back. She bit his tongue so hard, she drew blood. She was not satisfied with simply being on her back, either. She rolled over so that he could take her on her side, ramming himself up deeper and deeper until both of them were in a blinding frenzy that demanded completion. But Skye held out for several more minutes, inflicting his scorching tongue on her mouth, her throat, her breasts, continuing to plumb her hot, silken depths until they both exploded in a delirium of satisfaction that left her literally crying with pleasure, and him doing the same kind of wild bucking and grinding that she'd been doing earlier.

And then they fell spent next to each other. But they did not lay there long because just as she was about to start talking again, Fargo brought her to him so that they lay face-to-face. And then he parted her wet inner thighs and inserted himself into her once again.

"You feel even bigger than you did a few minutes ago," she said.

"I've been outriding a wagon train for quite a while," he said, as his pelvis began to find its preferred rhythm again. "The only chance I had for sex was with this female bear. And she told me she was engaged to be married."

Doris giggled. "Such a big man, and you're funny, too. I'm afraid I'm going to just have to fall in love with you, Skye."

He wanted to say, Let's not spoil a good thing here. But why ruin the moment for her? He was getting what he wanted and so was she.

They didn't finish for another half hour . . .

*   *   *

A misty rain began to fall, making the lamplight streaming from the casino windows look as rich as the highest carat gold. The light promised warmth, a relaxing beer, conversation.

He was all set to have himself a relaxing time, when he saw a woman in a wheelchair being pushed down the boardwalk. She was a slight figure wrapped in a cape and cowl and her wheelchair was being pushed by a large woman dressed likewise. The large woman pushed with care and expertise, navigating the boardwalk skillfully, seeming to know each and every bump and jag in the lumber.

The woman in the wheelchair grew more impossibly beautiful the nearer she got, her aristocratic face framed perfectly by the cowl, long red hair spilling from the same frame. The way she looked about so hungrily—as if she'd never seen civilization before—told Fargo that she didn't get out all that much and was most appreciative of being among human beings, even on a misty night, even when most of the human beings were inside saloons and the lone casino.

When the chair pulled abreast of Fargo, he tipped his hat and said, "Good evening, ma'am."

The woman's smile was stunning in its power over Fargo. She was one of the most elegant creatures Fargo had ever seen. "Good evening, sir. It's a lovely night, isn't it?"

Fargo noticed how the buxom Mexican woman pushing the wheelchair rolled her eyes, as if she had just heard the words of an imbecile. "Miss Fiona thinks tromping around in the rain and the mud is a lovely way to spend an evening."

"Spend some time in this chair," Fiona said, not unkindly. "And you'll think the same way I do." Then she addressed Fargo again. "You must come from a land of giants."

Fargo smiled. "I guess I am a pretty good size."

"And handsome," Fiona said.

"Thank you."

"When I still had my legs—" Her eyes fell to the dead things beneath the blanket she had wrapped around the lower half of her body. "When I still had my legs, you

8

were exactly the kind of man I would have asked to go dancing with me."

"And I would have been happy to oblige."

"Is anybody except me getting wet?" Fiona's companion asked.

"The rain is picking up isn't it," Fargo said, looking to the sky. "But then again, such lovely company is worth an extra drop or two."

Fiona laughed. "My name is Fiona Caine, by the way." She offered a slender hand and they shook. "And you are?"

"Skye Fargo's the name. I just stopped over for a night or two in Cumberland. I've always heard that you could have a lot of fun here."

"Well," Fiona said, "that used to be true." Then— the first hint that being in her wheelchair had left her bitter—"But a lot of things used to be true, Mr. Fargo."

"I wear 'Skye' a lot better than I do 'Mr. Fargo.' "

She scanned his formidable, buck-skinned body again. "Yes, I imagine that's true." Then she nodded to the casino a block away. "You might try the Ruby Rooster. That's a very nice place, I hear."

"Yes," laughed the Mexican woman. "And she's not at all prejudiced."

Fargo started to ask the woman what she'd meant by her remark but then Fiona said, "I guess it is getting a little too damp out here tonight. Maybe it's time to head back home."

"Well, I'm glad I got to meet you."

"I wish we could've met before—" She left the sentence unfinished. "Just my luck to run into a man like you when I'm stuck in this damned contraption."

Thunder rattled heaven and earth. Fargo saw how Fiona trembled at its power. She looked like a frightened little girl in that moment. Such a pity that she was forced to live out her life in a wheelchair. Fargo wondered what had put her there.

"Good evening, Skye," she said, taking her leave of him.

He watched till the wheelchair was well down the boardwalk before turning back to the lights of the saloon and the lone casino. This was a strange town. Why would two casinos be dark? What had happened here? And could it possibly have anything to do with what had put a beautiful woman in a wheelchair?

By the time Fargo neared the Ruby Rooster Casino, the protestors had dispersed. As he aproached the entrance he saw the outline of a man. He lay near the boardwalk, facedown in the mud. He could have been asleep or dead. Hypocrisy never ceased to amaze him. The protestors had been too busy trying to think for consenting adults to notice someone who might actually need some help.

Fargo bent down and turned the man's head toward the light. A drunkard. The man's face was gaunt but his skin was puffy and webbed with broken blood vessels. His teeth were small, rotted, fetid things. And one of his eyes was ringed with a shiner that would do a boxer proud.

Fargo saw that a couple of photographs had spilled from the man's pocket. He picked them up and stared at them in the faint light. A beautiful young woman sat in a wheelchair in each of the pictures. The woman he'd just met. Fiona. Why would a derelict like this have her photographs?

"What's your name?" Fargo asked.

"You gonna hit me?"

"I asked you what your name was."

The man patted the pocket of his ragged, muddy jacket. "Hey, did you steal my bottle?"

"Yeah. And I took all the money you had in your pockets, too. And all the diamonds."

"I had money? And diamonds?" The man sounded confused. Sarcasm was wasted on him.

"What's your name?"

"It's Philly. Why?"

"Because you're going to get pneumonia out here like this, Philly. You belong anywhere?" By now, Fargo knew that he'd stumbled across—literally—the town drunk.

The melancholy, middle-aged face, from which fear never quite left, said, "Not so's you'd notice."

Fargo grabbed the man and pulled him to his feet. He

slid his arm through Philly's and half-dragged the man back to the hotel where he was staying.

He pushed the photographs back in the man's pocket. "How do you know Fiona?"

"You keep your hands off her. She's my friend." He slurred his words badly.

"I just asked how you knew her."

"That's none of yer damned business." Philly stumbled. "Where you takin' me?" He was, like many drunkards, subject to fits of terror. Where the hell did he think Fargo was taking him? To the dark woods where monsters waited to feast on drunks?

When they reached the hotel, Fargo dragged Philly across the lobby. The desk clerk had already spotted Philly. The clerk looked as if he wanted to hide. A couple of the drummers with their stogies started laughing at the sight of the drunkard. He was obviously familiar to them.

"Yes?" the clerk said. A bellboy who had to be at least sixty years old watched Philly with sad interest. The man knew what it was like to be a laughing stock.

"He needs a room," Fargo said, laying enough cash on the counter for one night's lodging.

The clerk made a clucking sound. "Mr. Fargo, you're a welcome guest here. But if I let Philly stay here—" The aged clerk looked at the drummers. They were all smirking. "Why, I'd lose my job."

"Well," Fargo said, "I'm going to lose my temper if you don't. He needs a hot bath and a room and his clothes washed. I'm pretty sure I saw all those things advertised on your sign outside."

"Yes, but—"

One of the jokers reading his newspaper in a lobby chair said, "Yeah, Earl and you personally got to give Philly his bath."

The other jokers, being jokers, laughed heartily at the man's brilliant wit.

"I can't do it, sir. I don't want to wake the manager to ask—"

"He lives here on the premises?"

"Why, yes, sir. But he's probably asleep by now and—"

Fargo didn't wait for him to finish. "What's his room number?"

"Why, Room 8 but—"

Fargo led Philly over to a chair. He spread several layers of newspaper on the chair, even on the arm cushions. Then he sat Philly down. In the clear light of the lobby, Philly looked like some kind of mud monster, a beast up from the swamps.

"You wait here," Fargo said. "You understand?"

Dazed, Philly glanced around.

Fargo didn't wait for him to respond.

He went back over to the clerk. "Anything happens to him, I'm holding you responsible. Understand?"

The clerk frowned. "But I can't—"

"Sure you can," Fargo said, "sure you can."

The hotel hallway, lighted by flickering candles in sconces, was narrow and filled with the noise of middle-aged men as eleven o'clock at night approached—belches, coughs, farts, curses, lonely bedsprings, even mumbled prayers—and the smells were also fitting: commodes, cigars, cigarettes, whiskey, sweat, sleep, and the minor illnesses that accrue to drummers and peddlers who spend their lives on the road.

He found Room 8 and knocked softly. When he didn't get any response, he knocked several times more, each time with less and less civility, until he was finally pounding.

He felt pretty stupid when the door finally opened and there stood a blind man of ancient visage and leathery skin. "I was asleep."

"Look, I'm sorry, sir, but I'm having some trouble with your desk clerk."

The blind man, who wore a white cotton night shirt, seemed to be peering at Fargo with milky dead eyes. "A lot of people have trouble with Earl. But he's my cousin. He's not a bad sort when you get to know him."

"You know a man named Philly?"

"Everybody in town knows Philly. He's a most unfortunate man." The gent spoke in a tender voice that was barely a whisper. He sounded like some sort of mystic-seer shuck artist in a carnival. He smelled of ointment. "How may I help you, sir?"

"I've got a little money ahead. I was doing some out-riding that paid pretty smart wages. I thought I'd spread a little of it around. I don't like to see people in the gutter."

"And you would like Earl to do what, sir?"

"Get Philly fixed up with a bath and a room for the night."

"Philly," the old man said.

"That's what I said."

"The town drunk."

"That's what I figured. My name's Skye Fargo, by the way."

"The Trailsman?"

"Yeah, that's what some folks call me, anyway."

The old man smiled. "You sound embarrassed by that name."

"It gets in the way sometimes."

"Earl reads me stories about you from time to time. I've heard that you were a fighter and a lover, Mister Fargo, but I hadn't heard you were a saint."

Fargo shrugged. "I just don't like the idea of a town that lets a man lie in the mud that way."

"Then you've come to the wrong town, Mister Fargo. Cumberland isn't much in the way of heart. Or soul, for that matter."

"There aren't any churches?"

"There's a Reverend Amis. You probably saw his pickets out in front of the last of our casinos. But he isn't a very admirable character, I'm afraid."

Fargo remembered Philly sitting in the lobby. "I brought Philly here."

"To the hotel?"

Fargo nodded. "Yes."

A sly smile touched the old man's mouth. "Poor Earl. I'll bet he nearly had a heart attack."

Fargo laughed. "Pretty close."

"You'll have to be responsible for Philly. I don't have the manpower to be chasing him all over the hotel."

"Given how drunk he is, a hot bath and a clean bed will be about the only thing you'll be out. And I'll pick up the tab for that and anything else."

"Then you tell Earl that it's all right with me."

"I appreciate this."

Fargo hurried back to the lobby.

He was gone. Philly was gone.

Earl was leaning on the desk talking to two of the guests who'd been reading newspapers and getting their nightly dose of nicotine.

Fargo went up to the desk. "Where's Philly?"

"Gone."

"Gone where?"

Earl shook his head. "I tried to stop him. But he just got up and ran out the door."

The other two, who'd been smirking sarcastically the whole time Fargo had been in the lobby before, were now somber.

"Poor bastard," said one of them. "It was like he kind of come to for a minute—his head jerked up and he looked around—and then he just kinda spooked."

"Yessir," said the other, "that's just what he done. Spooked. Like a horse. And just took off right out that there door there."

The front door. Philly probably had spooked. Couldn't believe he was supposed to be in any place as respectable as this one. And just ran out the door.

"I'm going to find him," Fargo said.

"He kin of yours or somethin', Mister Fargo?" one man asked.

But Fargo had already taken off.

"Hey, are you the Trailsman?" the other man called. He sounded like a kid awed by some storybook character.

But Fargo didn't have time to answer any questions. He wanted to find Philly. It was frustrating. You try and do a good deed for somebody and they won't even accept it, Fargo thought.

Being a saint wasn't as easy as it looked from the outside.

The first thing you had to learn was how to make people hold still . . .

Philly had vanished into the fog. Fargo spent twenty minutes looking for him. He'd made good money outriding and thought it would be nice to do something decent for a poor soul like Philly. But his saint period was short-lived. There were too many things he wanted to do for himself. He'd tried to do his good deed, and the hell with it . . .

Three times a night, one of the deputies checked the hotel registration books. The sheriff always wanted to know who was staying in his town . . .

If you didn't know what Sheriff Tom Bradshaw had done with his life, all you had to do was look at the east wall of his office. There you saw clippings from a couple dozen newspapers recounting his exploits as a town-tamer. His name appeared in many different books about the so-called Wild West as well. Bradshaw, in his prime years a powerfully built man with a shock of red hair that could light the darkest cave, was often quoted as saying "I would've been an outlaw, but I was too lazy. Robbing banks is hard work."

The flattering newspaper accounts invariably used the word "hero" a great deal. Bradshaw enjoyed these pieces well enough, but the ones he really liked were the ones that called him "one of the deadliest men in the West" and "a killer as fierce as any outlaw he ever faced." Some men liked to think of themselves as good, some men liked to think of themselves as bad. Bradshaw simply liked to think of himself as dangerous.

"Sheriff."

It was nearing midnight and Bradshaw was still in his office. This was where he spent his nights since his wife had up and died on him three years ago. That's how he thought of it. Up and died on him. Escaped would probably be a better word. She'd run away three times, sick of how he ruled her life, but he'd always dragged her back and convinced her to give him another chance. Now he had no place to go at night, so he ate in the café, came back to his office, slapped around some of the more unruly drunks, and then sat in his office, reading the magazines he subscribed to or looking over the old clippings about himself.

He looked up from his reading. "Yes," he said to the young man who had just come in.

"There's a man in town I thought you should know

15

about." The kid deputy spoke carefully. You did not want to displease Bradshaw.

"What man?"

"I thought maybe you'd heard of him."

"Boy," Bradshaw said, the springs in his chair squeaking as he leaned forward, a scowl widening his moon face. "You better come to the point."

"The Trailsman is what they call him."

"Skye Fargo?"

"Yessir. Skye Fargo."

"What's he doin' here?"

"I don't rightly know, sir. All I know is he checked into the hotel. That's where he is now. He was helpin' Philly."

"Helpin' Philly? Why would he do a thing like that? Who the hell would want to help Philly?"

"I guess he felt sorry for him or somethin', Sheriff." He hesitated. "I just thought you'd like to know, sir."

Bradshaw's face softened. "Sorry I snapped at you."

"Yessir."

"You're doing a good job, son."

This sudden change did not surprise the deputy. This was how Bradshaw was. Nice and considerate; angry and violent. You could never tell which he was going to be. Sometimes he changed from moment to moment. Those who knew him well always talked about how, sometimes, when he was drunk, he would tear up and talk about what a terrible husband he'd been, how he'd driven his wife to an early grave, and how he'd been an even worse father, driving his son away and never hearing from him again.

"Thank you, sir."

"You know I don't want Fargo in my town."

"Yessir, I kind've figured that."

"No gunnies. That's why we don't have trouble here."

"Well, except for those murders, sir."

"Are you making fun of me, son?"

"No, sir, I just meant that we still haven't figured out who killed—"

"Well, I will figure that out, son. And then we'll go back to being peaceful."

"Yessir."

"How's your wife doing, son?"

He smiled. "I'll be glad when she has the baby."

"You be sure and invite me to the christening."

"Oh, I will, sir, you can count on that."

"I appreciate you telling me about Fargo, son."

"Yessir. Well, I better get back to making my rounds."

Fargo, Bradshaw thought. *Skye Fargo.* Very big rep. Pretty much known throughout the West. The kind of man who could make an aging sheriff look mighty bad if anything happened. He might be faster than the aging sheriff; smarter. With ties to both the Army and the Indian nations, Fargo was known to have a lot of skills the average white man just couldn't claim. Just one more thing an aging sheriff had to worry about.

So what could an aging sheriff do? If he was smart, anyway. He would force Skye Fargo out of town before the man could do any harm to said sheriff's reputation. That's what the smart aging sheriff would do. And while Bradshaw had been accused of many things in his life, stupidity wasn't one of them.

2

The Ruby Rooster was the fanciest setup Fargo had seen outside of Denver. No crude furnishings here. The casino boasted a long bar, dining area, poker tables, and all of the gambling devices had been teamstered or trained in from St. Louis or Chicago. The girls—the quickest way to tell what kind of establishment you were dealing with—were young, clean, attractive. Maybe not great beauties but definitely attractive. The various croupiers were all dressed identically—white shirts with red sleeve garters, red cummerbunds, black trousers—and each wore a large and obvious Navy Colt holstered to his leg. The murals of painted ladies were more suggestive than intimate. And the four-piece band played sweet songs as often as it played toe-tappers. This wasn't quite the Barbary Coast, in terms of style, but it sure came damned close.

Fargo got his beer, which was fine, and a lot of conversation, which wasn't fine. The place crawled with drummers. And nobody could yak like drummers. It didn't seem to matter to them what they were yakking about just as long as their mouths kept making noise.

Then Fargo saw her and couldn't stop staring. Her dark-haired good looks demanded instant and lasting attention, especially set inside the low-cut white evening gown she wore. Just a glimpse of her stirred his groin. He had gone too long without a woman before today, and then to see one like this—one who was part princess and part expensive harlot—turned him into an animal in bad need of companionship. A man never knew when a dry spell might pass, and Fargo learned at an early age to quench his thirst while he had the chance. Doris seemed a long ways back in the distance now.

But neither the woman's good looks, her gown, or Fargo's own randiness was the issue here. No, the issue was the startling resemblance she bore to the woman in the wheelchair, Fiona Caine, and the photograph Philly had had on him tonight and had clung to with almost pathetic desperation. Why would Fiona Caine be photographed in a wheelchair? And why would Philly have that photograph of her?

"You know who that woman is?" Fargo asked the drummer who'd been gnawing on his ear. The man had a round, freckled face with apple cheeks and an overbite. He looked like a ventriloquist's dummy.

"She's a beauty, ain't she? Just about the purtiest gal I ever seen. Noelle, her name is. Noelle Caine. How'd you like to slip her the old porker, huh?"

Fargo watched as Noelle began to pass among the tables, hands eagerly grabbing at her, like the hands of peasants trying to steal pieces of food. She had an amused eye for the whole show.

Fargo wondered how long it had taken Fiona to jump out of her wheelchair, get dolled up and run across the muddy streets to the casino here. Maybe she liked to play tricks. Maybe The Ruby Rooster liked to play games the way those places on the Barbary Coast did. Maybe Fiona Caine liked to pretend she was twins and titillate all the lusty drinkers in her place with her dual personality.

"She's got a sister just as good-lookin'," the drummer said. "Fact is, they're identical twins."

"I'll say."

The drummer shook his head. "Yeah, Fiona. I always liked Fiona a little better, myself. She owned half this casino and worked here, too. She wasn't as haughty as Noelle here. Then she up and got herself shot about three years ago."

"They ever find out who did it or why?"

"Nope." The drummer smiled with evil intent. "Some fellas think Noelle did it."

"Her own sister? Why?"

19

"This was about the time I moved here. So I don't know the whole history. But it seems Noelle got jealous of the attention her husband started payin' to Fiona."

As Noelle swept by, majestic in her vanity, she let her dark eyes rest upon Skye Fargo's face. She was clearly intrigued by the big man's rough but handsome features and by the image of him in damp buckskins. The oiled holster tied gunny-style to his leg didn't hurt the slightly dangerous air he projected either, especially not since it was filled with a formidable Colt.

Then she was gone, leaving the impression that someone very important had passed by, favoring all the little people with her divine attention.

For a number of reasons, Fargo was taken with the woman he'd just seen. He wanted her sexually, that was for sure. But he was also caught up in the mystery of her. Two sisters who were virtually identical. And one becomes so jealous of the other that she shoots her?

Fargo loved campfire tales. And here was a great one. Two twins run a casino together. One gets jealous of the other. Shoots her. Paralyzes her for life. Even if it hadn't happened that way, it should have.

Fargo, flush from his outriding job, spent half an hour trying his luck.

The Ruby Rooster was well-appointed. Rochester lamps gave the three large rooms a shadowy elegance. There were tables for poker, faro, roulette, red and black, black jack, high dice. Drinks were served from a bar overseen by a portrait of a giant ruby-colored rooster.

Fargo won a little, lost a little. A gambler he was not. Women could get him going; and once in a while hard liquor could do the same. But the truth was, with the exception of the occasional poker hand, gambling quickly dulled for him. The repetition of it proved quickly monotonous.

He was just leaving the faro table when he became aware of a situation that had been developing over the past few minutes.

A huge Swede had grabbed one of the croupiers and had stabbed the barrel of a Navy Colt against his head, taking him hostage. "I want to see Noelle!" the Swede shouted. "And if I don't see her, this man'll be dead before he hits the ground."

The Swede and the croupier stood between two of the gambling rooms in an open area. The Swede had been smart enough to grab the man in front of a wall. Nobody could sneak up behind him.

The gamblers and the croupiers stopped playing their various games. The shifting haze of tobacco smoke seemed to hold as still as the human beings.

Noelle, composed, quiet, strode over to the Swede and said, "Nordberg, this is insane. You're just going to get yourself tossed in jail. You've got a wife and six kids to feed. You'd better start thinking about them before I get Sheriff Bradshaw over here."

Nordberg was dressed in a flat black hat, a sheepskin jacket, a red flannel shirt, and brown wool homesteader pants reenforced at the knees and seat with buckskin. The gun he had pressed to the croupier's temple shook slightly.

"You killed my brother Gunnar," Nordberg said. "And if you don't admit it right now, I'll kill this here man of yours." He spoke in an accent that mixed Swedish and English.

"I didn't kill Gunnar," Noelle said softly. "But I'll say I did if you'll let Sam Pines here go. He's got two kids of his own. The girl isn't even two yet. Let me take his place."

"I don't got nothin' against this here fella," Nordberg said. "I just want you to go to trial for killin' my brother. And those two other men." His words had begun to slur. He was drunk, which made everything much worse.

Fargo noticed that the longer they talked, the more Nordberg moved to his right, pushing Sam out ahead of him so that the two men faced Noelle almost directly. The protection Nordberg had gotten from being against the wall was no longer so great.

Fargo hadn't strayed far from the bar so that now, when he moved, he was behind Nordberg.

He knew he was about to risk not only his life but Sam's, too. Nordberg obviously wasn't a killer—didn't really plan to shoot Sam—but given his drunkenness and his grief over his dead brother, he was a danger to everybody, including himself.

Fargo knew that even if he were to backshoot the Swede, the man's gun could still fire and kill Sam.

There was only one possible way to safely extricate the revolver from Nordberg's hand and he'd need one hell of a lot of luck to do it.

He slipped off his boots, crouched down and took a coin from his pocket. He had faced many similar situations like this when he tracked people. More than once he'd been hired to capture them, not kill them. He knew he could distract Nordberg for at best a few seconds. And in that momentary window of time, he would have to make his move.

The men along the bar watched him silently as he haunch-walked his way along the wall to where Nordberg and Sam stood. Noelle watched him, too, but her eyes never betrayed Fargo to Nordberg.

"He took a lot of your money," Nordberg was saying. "That's why you killed him. Killed them all. They won a lot of money at your tables and you needed to get it back. So you waited till you had a chance and then you backshot 'em like the terrible bitch you are!"

Nordberg was working himself into a frenzy. This would make him more dangerous than ever. This was when men did the crazy drunken things they'd wake up in the morning—usually in a jail cell—to face with remorse and disbelief.

But this was also an opportunity for Fargo. A man this worked up—and this drunk—was not likely to hear the incidental noises around him. And Skye Fargo was trying not to make any noise at all.

"C'mon now, Nordberg," Noelle said. "Let him go and you can have me. I don't have any children depending on me. You can do whatever you want to with me."

Fargo was impressed not only by her calm but her courage.

The time to move was now.

He came out of his crouch. Took two steps forward

22

so that he was close enough to the Swede to smell the harshness of liquor and the sweat of rage on him.

He bounced the coin on the lower part of Nordberg's neck, just above the shoulders.

The reaction was instant for both men. Nordberg, as if bee-stung, flinched and turned in profile for just a moment. And Fargo leaped upon him, his hand already finding and closing on Nordberg's gun wrist, knocking the revolver away from Sam's temple. Sam was instinctively shrewd enough to dive for the floor. Fargo and Nordberg struggled for possession of the gun until Fargo brought a knee up so savagely into the lowest part of Nordberg's spine. The Swede was thrown into the wall so violently that you could hear his nose shatter. Snapping bone makes an unforgettable sound all its own.

The Swede was on the floor, sobbing as only a man can, grieving over his brother.

There was a collective sense of relief. Bodies were no longer tense. Hands slipped away from holsters. Drinks were brought to lips again.

"The poor bastard," an onlooker said.

To one of her bouncers, Noelle said, "Get him cleaned up, give him some coffee and then see that he gets home all right."

"No sheriff?" Fargo said.

Noelle looked at him with great interest. "If I was in his spot, I might do the same thing." Then she put out her hand. "Noelle Kingsley. How about having a drink in my office with me?"

Fargo grinned. "I guess I've had worse offers in my day."

3

A Rochester lamp cast deep shadows over the small, square room that was half-office and half-salon. The north side of the room held two oak file cabinets, a desk with an oil lamp and straightback chairs for visitors. The south side held a divan, a Persian rug, a small well-stocked bar, and several miniature paintings of Noelle's face from different angles.

"A little vain, I realize," she said, as she fixed a drink. "But the artist was traveling through and he was broke and I thought I should get my money's worth."

"You've got a face well worth painting."

"Thank you, Skye."

She brought Fargo his drink, sat primly on the edge of the divan next to him. He tried not to be quite so aware of her sexuality, which was subtle but certain. The slopes of her breasts encased in her low-cut gown were hard to stop gaping at. She was slender but sumptuously built.

"What's the scent of the incense?"

"Sandalwood," she said. "It's beautiful, isn't it?"

Fargo smiled. "It's more than that. It's downright seductive."

"Good," she laughed, "then it's doing its job."

They sipped their drinks. Fargo was a beer man, but this was excellent sour mash.

"You saved Sam's life out there," she said. "Maybe mine."

"Oh, I don't think Nordberg would've killed anybody."

"But you couldn't be sure of that."

Fargo shrugged. "Well, if I hadn't stepped in, somebody else would have."

"I didn't notice either of my bouncers rushing to do the job."

"Then I'd get new bouncers."

She got up suddenly. Walked over to a window. Stared out. He sensed turmoil in her. He still wondered what the scene with the Swede had been about. The man had seemed deeply aggrieved. His brother was dead and he blamed Noelle.

"I've tried to get new bouncers. But nobody wants to work here. In fact, I'm sure Sam—who's my best croupier—will be quitting after tonight. And I certainly can't blame him."

"This is a gambling town. There must be other bouncers."

She scoffed. "A gambling town? A year ago, there were three casinos here. Now there's just this one. And at the rate things are going, I won't be here much longer, either."

"When I rode in, I heard gunfire. I figured cowboys were having some fun. The way they usually do in towns like this."

"That is what you heard, Skye. But there's less and less of it as time goes on."

He decided now was a logical time to ask his question. "The Swede tonight—did that have anything to do with two of the casinos folding?"

She laughed bitterly. "Funny you should ask, Skye. The Swede tonight is exactly what I'm up against. And again, I don't blame him one bit for thinking I murdered his brother."

"How about explaining all this to me from the beginning? It'd make a lot more sense."

She came over and took his glass, bending low as she did so. She caught him staring at her breasts and said, "I like a man with good taste."

She got them fresh drinks and then told her story.

Cumberland was a hub of trade and fun for a large chunk of this part of Oregon. The casino owners who set up business here weren't the fly-by-night types. Most had families. All had set up shop here with an eye to spending the rest of their lives in this area. So they took their jobs very, very seriously. And rode herd on every single aspect of their businesses.

They bemoaned the escalating price of liquor, tobacco, good playing cards, and the wages of croupiers these days. So much for the glamour of casinos. These were businessmen just like any others, trying to make a profit.

But they made their profits in relatively clean ways. Whoring was kept strictly to the casino area. The drinks were honest and so were the games. The casinos even tried to cut workingmen off if they were spending too much of their paychecks. A couple of the casino owners went to church on Sundays and didn't want to face enraged wives whose children had been deprived of food, shelter, and clothing because Daddy had lost it all at the faro table.

Again, the idea was to stay here in the good graces of the community.

Then the good Reverend Amis Tyler came to Cumberland and everything changed. The hard-core churchgoers had never been pleased that the casinos were here. They didn't seem to understand that if the casinos went away, they'd take the town with it. Gambling was Cumberland's principal industry. Most of the church-going people were of mainstream religions, though, and were decent people, and believed in live and let live.

But the Bible-thumpers remained small in number and zero in influence until Amis became good friends with the local sheriff and the local newspaper editor and began putting a lot of pressure on the casinos to go elsewhere. Torchlight protests ensued. Bible-spouting ladies in bonnets began standing in front of casinos and handing out pamphlets on the sin of gambling. Amis even got small groups of children to stand in front of the casinos and sing hymns as high rollers and their ladies tried to work their way inside.

One of the casino owners gave up early in frustration. The second owner was driven out of business by angry gamblers who found that three of his games had been rigged. Only after the owner had fled town were whispers heard about one of the owner's croupier's working undercover for Amis. The croupier had rigged the games in such a way that it looked as if his employer had done it.

"With me, there's a new tactic," Noelle said. "In the past month, two customers of mine were murdered after they'd won a lot of money here. On their way home, somebody robbed them and killed them. Naturally, it looks like I did it."

"To get your money back? That's why you were supposed to have killed them?"

"Sure."

"And so, naturally, that's cut down on the number of your customers?"

"Business is way off. And the newspaper is running editorials hinting that I should be indicted for two murders."

Just then there was a knock on the door. "Excuse me, Skye," Noelle said.

She answered the knock. A croupier stood there. Whatever he said to Noelle was lost in the din of the casino. She nodded and closed the door.

When she came back, worry tightened her face.

"Trouble?" Fargo said.

"Somebody's winning big at black jack tonight."

"You have enough to cover it?"

She stood at the window again, leaning against the wall this time. Fargo wondered about her relationship with Fiona. About the rumors that Noelle had shot her sister. He also wondered about the husband the sisters had allegedly argued over. Where was he? But now wasn't the time to ask such questions.

"Money's not the trouble," Noelle said. "The casino still has plenty of money. Fiona and I were always careful to keep a cash reserve." A bitter smile. "I'm sure you've heard about my sister Fiona. That's another story about me they like to tell in this town. That I shot her in the back and crippled her for life." She shook her head. Fargo noted that she didn't exactly deny that she'd shot Fiona. "Anyway, money's not the trouble. I can ride out a storm for quite a while. But if one more of my customers gets killed and robbed—"

"That's what you're worried about? That the one who's winning big tonight may not get home safely?"

27

"Very worried, Skye." She pushed away from the wall and, turning to Fargo, said "Would you see that he gets home safely, Skye? I'd make it worth your while." She came over and sat next to him. She was too subtle a woman to make any kind of obvious move, but in this moment the air was suddenly charged with a message her entire body was sending.

"Listen, Noelle. I just came to town here for a little relaxation. I'm not sure I—"

And then she was in his arms. And then her seeking, urgent mouth was open on his. As he leaned over to take her in his arms, her hand slipped across his buckskins to find his thigh. A groan filled Fargo's throat as he slowly leaned her back on her couch. And that was when—

—the door opened.

No warning whatsoever. If there'd been a key scraping against a lock, Fargo hadn't heard it.

The tall, slender man standing there looked like most of the gamblers who'd worked the Southern riverboats before the war. The dark suit, white frilly shirt, string tie, red brocaded vest. The only difference was that the riverboat boys preferred to hide their weapons. This handsome specimen chose to wear his strapped down against his leg.

"I thought I told you to turn your key in," Noelle snapped, as she and Fargo moved away from each other. They were like two school kids who'd been caught playing naughty games behind the barn.

The man smirked. His aristocratic face conveyed nothing more than amusement. "I must've forgotten. But I have to say, you two put on a pretty nice show. You could go a little further. I wouldn't mind, as long as I got to watch."

Noelle got up, charged across the room. Put her hand out. Palm up. "The key."

"I guess I must've lost it."

She slapped him with bone-cracking fury. "The key. Now."

"That's one thing you'll have to be careful of, Mister Fargo," the man said, affecting a droll voice to hide his embarrassment at being slapped so hard. "My wife has a terrible temper."

"Your ex-wife," she said.

"Not quite yet, darling. Not quite yet. The divorce isn't final for another month." He smirked again, this time in Fargo's direction. "When the croupier told me that my wife was in her office with Skye Fargo, I thought to myself that Noelle is coming up in the world. You're a very prominent man, Mr. Fargo. I'm Rick Kingsley, by the way."

"Get out, Rick." She didn't wait for him to move. For a woman of such diminutive size, she had no trouble shoving him back across the threshold. "You know I don't want you in my casino. And tonight I'm going to make that official. I'm putting everybody on notice that you're not to be let in under any circumstances. Do you understand?"

She slammed the door with the same viciousness she'd slapped him with.

When she went over to pour more sour mash into her drink, she said, "I'm sorry for the interruption. We'll have to pick up where we left off some other time. Right now I'm not in the mood."

He saw in that moment how the various pressures in her life were starting to collapse in on her. She looked lonely and—for the first time—frightened. He got up and walked over to her.

He said, "That's the trouble with being a mule."

She looked up from her bitter thoughts. "What?"

"I'm a mule in harness. I don't know what to do with myself when I'm not working. Why don't we go out there and see how your big winner's coming along? If it looks like he might need a little help getting home, I'll be happy to oblige."

She set her drink down, slid her arms around him. Right now she needed the sense of security and comfort a big, hard man like Fargo could give her and he was happy to oblige. He found himself liking the woman. He just hoped that she hadn't actually tried to kill her sister.

4

They were just about to leave her office when a heavy knock landed on Noelle's door. She said, "Who is it?"

"Sheriff Bradshaw."

Her full mouth pursed. Obviously, Bradshaw wasn't a man she cared for. "There's no trouble now, Sheriff. Nordberg went on home. I don't want to file any charges."

"Open the door, Miss Noelle. And I mean now."

Fargo shrugged. There was no point in making Bradshaw's kind of lawman even angrier. Between their guns and their badges, they always had the upper hand. Fargo nodded to the door. She opened it.

Bradshaw was a giant ruin of a man. It was easy to imagine him young, or even in middle-aged, clearing out a saloon full of villains; or overseeing a hanging that was not, strictly speaking, legal. He was the Old West, when legal niceties weren't always the order of the day. He was, even given his round stomach and triple chins, an imposing man in his tall white Stetson, his rawhide jacket, and his outsize sheriff's badge. From his left hand dangled the smallest sawed-off shotgun Fargo had ever seen. In Bradshaw's massive hand, it looked like a toy.

"I'd like to use your office for a few minutes, Miss Noelle."

"For what purpose?"

"To talk to your man friend here." He made "man friend" sound like a very dirty thing to be.

"About what?" Noelle said.

"I'd say that's my business. Now you clear out."

Noelle started to argue again, and Fargo said, "I always enjoy meeting the duly appointed officials of the law, Noelle. Why don't you go have a drink?"

Fargo's sarcasm brought a grimace to Bradshaw's once-handsome face. He obviously didn't like phrases like "duly appointed officials of the law." He knew they were meant to make fun of him.

"You sure?" Noelle asked.

"I'll be fine."

"I don't like this, Sheriff," she said to Bradshaw as she picked up her drink to take with her.

"I don't reckon you do," Bradshaw said. "And I don't give a damn, either."

"You're always such a gentleman, Sheriff," Noelle cooed sarcastically. "I guess that's why everybody likes you so much."

She had barely closed the door when Bradshaw made his move. Toylike though his small sawed-off might be, when he slammed the butt of it into Fargo's midsection, Fargo did exactly what Bradshaw wanted him to do—folded in half and fought a strong desire to vomit.

Not that Bradshaw stopped there. Men like him never did. He was staking out his territory—the entire town of Cumberland, in his case—the way a predatory animal does, and he obviously wanted Fargo to understand that he was in charge of it and that if he did anything to displease Bradshaw, Fargo would be treated to even more severe punishment.

He cracked Fargo on the side of the head with the butt of the sawed-off. Fargo responded by sinking to his knees, dazed. At which point, as a finale, Bradshaw lashed out with his right foot and planted it boot deep into Fargo's stomach. This time, fighting the vomit wasn't so easy.

Fargo groped blindly for something to hold on to, found the edge of the desk and gripped it with trembling fingers.

"Now, if I was to run you out of town tonight, Mister Fargo, I'd catch holy shit from the town council. They've got all these legal codes they worry about. They'd ask me why I threw you out of Cumberland, and I'd say because he's a gunny who's come here for trouble. And then they'd tell me about all the things all those newspaper boys have written about you over the years. The Trailsman and that whole line of bullshit. And no matter what I'd tell them—how by bein' a lawman all these years, I can recognize a snake as soon as I see one—they'd blame me for not treatin' you right, not even givin' you a chance in our nice little burg here. So you know what I'm gonna do, Fargo? I'm gonna let you stay around here for a few days. And let you do what comes natural. Because we both know what that is, don't we? That's gettin' in trouble. And that's when I'm gonna nail your ass to the wall, Fargo. Hell, you might even give me the opportunity to shoot you. And believe me, that'd be an opportunity I sure wouldn't pass up. Now we understand each other, Mister Fargo."

The boot came swift and sure out of nowhere. It caught Fargo just below the ribs. This time, he couldn't take it anymore. He sprang from his kneeling position, hurled himself upon the bigger man and drove him all the way back to the wall. The entire office shook. A few knickknacks dropped to the floor.

Fargo smashed three savage fists into Bradshaw's midsection. It was now the lawman's turn to fold in half. But Fargo wasn't done. He snatched the sawed-off from Bradshaw's hand and returned the favor—slicing the butt of the sawed-off right into Bradshaw's sternum. The man went pale, bug-eyed, frozen there for a moment as if his entire body had shut down. The blow must have been tremendous. And then suddenly he was animated again, cursing at Fargo, starting toward him.

The door flew open. Noelle stood in the frame, pointing a .45 at Bradshaw. "Had your fun, Sheriff?"

The lawman hadn't crumpled up, but he was having a difficult time regulating his breathing. It came out in ragged gasps; wet, nasal wheezes.

Fargo handed him his sawed-off. "It was nice meeting you, Sheriff."

"The fun's only started, Fargo. Believe me."

He glared first at Noelle and then at Fargo. He straightened up, righted his badge, which had canted to the left, and then composed himself as much as possible.

He left without another word.

"You just made an enemy, Skye," she said. "A bad one."

Fargo set about collecting himself. He wanted a beer.

The man had red whiskers turning gray, and a boozy button nose and a small squinched-up face. He looked like a rabbit that had climbed into a checkered shirt and a vest. He also had a grin so big that only one of two things could have inspired it—lust or greed. Given the fact that nearly four thousand dollars in greenbacks sat in front of him at the black jack table, Fargo assumed it was the latter that made him so happy.

Fargo and Noelle stood off to the side of the crowd that had gathered to watch the man play.

"His name's McCarey," Noelle said. "Rufe McCarey. He's a rancher and a bad drinker. He's always falling off his horse and breaking something. It'd be funny except he's got a sweet little wife who goes to Mass three times a week and prays that he doesn't kill himself."

"I imagine she'll appreciate the money, though."

"If he's smart enough to quit."

"You think he'll blow it?"

"A lot of them do." She smiled sadly. "It's funny, even though it's my money they're winning, a part of me wants to see them quit while they're ahead. They don't understand how the house works. And the house doesn't have to cheat to do it."

"You play long enough and the house wins."

"Exactly."

Fargo checked the casino out for any unduly suspicious faces. He was always surprised by how stupid most criminals were. They'd stand in a place like this scoping out the man they wanted to rob. And then they'd follow him right out the door and rob him. As if the people in the casino or saloon wouldn't remember them.

But he didn't see anybody like that. The professional gamblers who paid McCarey any attention at all looked amused more than anything. Nearly everybody gets to get lucky one night in his life. This was McCarey's night. No big deal to a real gambler. The other six people, who looked like workingmen and farmers, were McCarey's cheering section. They sounded and acted as if they were at a prize fight, urging him on not just with their voices but their whole bodies, waving their arms, hurrahing with their hats, even doing little dances. They got downright exuberant every time he beat the house.

"I don't see anybody, either," Noelle said.

"I should've figured you were checking them out, too."

"Whoever killed those other two men did it on the roads home. And I don't think they were in here at all. That's my hunch anyway. The killer was too smart for that."

"Then how did he find out who won the money?"

"Easy. People who gamble go from saloon to saloon. They talk about who's wining big and who's losing big. The killer could've heard about the big winners any number of places."

A roar of disappointment came from McCarey's cheering section.

"Aw, Rufe."

"Shit, Rufe."

"That's too bad, Rufe."

And then somebody said it: "Maybe you should think about quittin', Rufe. Just think how happy Josie'll be, you bring all that money home to her tonight."

Fargo watched McCarey's cartoon of a face. There were a lot of hard years in the severe lines of that face. A lot of struggle. A lot of discouragement.

Use your head, Fargo thought. *You've still got most of your money left. You could walk out of here with enough money to live on for three years if you lived right. And think of the smile you'd put on your wife's face. I'll bet she's worked out just as bad as you are, after all these years, Rufe. So use your head. Quit now.*

Rufe said to the croupier, "I'm gonna fold."

And his friends started slapping him on the back so hard, they were likely to crack his spine in several places. McCarey, all bowlegged and small-man wiry, eased off the stool at the table and started folding and stuffing the money in his pocket.

"I'm gonna buy every one of you boys a round," McCarey said. "And then I'm gonna head home and give this here money to Josie. Damn, I can see her smilin' now." The tears in his throat and eyes were obvious. Rufe McCarey seemed to be a pretty decent guy.

While his friends headed for the bar and the free round, Noelle said, "Rufe, could I talk to you a minute, please?"

McCarey turned to see who'd called him. "Oh, hi, Noelle."

"Could we talk a minute? I've got somebody I'd like you to meet."

Fargo watched the quick transformation on McCarey's face. His first response had been of pleasure when he'd turned to see that it was Noelle calling him. But now there was doubt—even apprehension—on the small man's face. It was clear he was remembering the two men who'd won big pots here only to be murdered and robbed on the way home.

McCarey came over, but Fargo watched as the man's hand began to hover closer to his six-shooter.

"Have you ever heard of Fargo, Rufe?" Noelle said.

"Sure. Who hasn't? Skye Fargo. Read about him several times."

"Well, if you'll agree, he's going to ride with you tonight when you go home."

McCarey took careful scrutiny of Fargo for the first time. "Well, hells bells, you're just like they describe in the newspaper."

Fargo smiled. "Don't believe everything you read—good or bad."

"Well, I'll be damned," McCarey said. "I win nearly four thousand dollars tonight. And I meet Skye Fargo."

"I don't want anything to happen to you," Noelle said. "So I'd like Skye to ride home with you."

McCarey grinned, his wiry whiskers shooting out on either side of his face, like the whiskers of a tom cat. "Skye Fargo ridin' along with me? I sure wouldn't turn that down."

"Well, why don't you go have that last drink with your friends, Rufe," Noelle said. "And then when you're ready to go, let me know and Skye'll be ready, too."

*   *   *

Fargo was about halfway to the livery stable when Rick Kingsley fell into step next to him. "Thought you might like a little company."

"Not your kind of company, Kingsley."

"I see you bought into Noelle's opinion of me."

"I formed my own opinion of you."

"Believe it or not, Fargo, I still care about the woman. I guess I just wasn't ready to settle down. But Noelle's not exactly the blushing-bride type, either."

Fargo stopped. To his right were the two shuttered casinos, darker even than the night itself. The fine mist continued to make every source of light glow ghostly. "What the hell do you want from me, anyway?"

"I want to know if she hired you."

"Why the hell should you care?"

"Because if she did, I want you to know I didn't have anything to do with killing those two customers of hers."

"Who said you did?"

Kingsley smiled. "She did, for one. And so did Fiona. It's sort of funny—now neither one of them want anything to do with me. That part I can live with. But being accused of killing somebody—that's not my kind of business, Fargo. I'm a gambler and that's all."

"You of course have alibis for the nights those two men were killed."

"Of course."

"And you can produce the people who'll swear you were with them?"

"If I need to."

"Meaning what?"

"Meaning," Rick Kingsley said, "that the lady I spent both nights with happens to be married to a very prestigious citizen in this little burg. A whole lot of lives would be ruined—including mine—if her very prestigious husband was ever to find out that his wife strays from time to time."

"Nobody else to back your alibi?"

"I don't usually invite people along on my trysts."

"Too bad. You could probably sell tickets."

"Let's get one thing straight, Fargo," Kingsley said. "I don't give a damn what you think of me. But my position in this town is precarious right now. A lot of

36

people would like to run me out of here. I'm perfectly willing to go, but I've got to get a little traveling cash before I do."

"Killing and robbing those two men could've gotten you a lot of cash. Maybe you're telling me all this just to cover your tracks."

Kingsley laughed. "I'm not that smart, Fargo. If I'd killed those two men and robbed them, I would've just kept on riding. There's no way I would've come back here."

"Maybe," Fargo said, "and maybe not. Now I need to be getting on to the livery."

James opened the door on Fargo's second knock. He wore a ragged sweater, a blue flannel shirt, work trousers.

"Sorry to wake you up," Fargo said.

James rubbed his face, yawned. "When I took this job, Mr. Clymer—man who owns this—told me it'd be easy at night. But you know somethin'? I get just about as much business at night as I do during the day, 'cept the reg'lars don't wake me up. They just come in and saddle up and ride out."

"That makes it easy for you, huh?" Fargo said, as James led him inside.

"Not really," James said. "I'm supposed to keep track of how the animals are. Takin' them in the middle of the night that way makes me nervous. I always have to get my gun out and make sure it's the rightful owner that's saddling up the animal. If I let the wrong person walk off with a horse, Mr. Clymer, he'd fire my colored ass in a minute. And then where would I be? I'd be livin' down with those hobos under the trestle bridge. They got their own little community down there, those fellas do."

"You know a man named Philly?"

"Sure do. Everybody does. That's where he lives most of the time," James said. "When he's got enough left in him to crawl down there, anyway."

"Sorry to wake you up," Fargo said and started saddling up the Ovaro.

James laughed. "It's all right. I needed to get up and empty the old sac, anyways."

*   *   *

When Fargo returned to the casino, he found a different atmosphere than the one he'd left. There was very little gambling going on. No player piano. No girls pushing drinks or dances. Most of the customers were watching the scene going on with McCarey and his friends.

McCarey stood inside a semi-circle of his drinking friends, facing off with Noelle.

"We'll take care of him ourselves," a beefy, bald man with several facial warts said.

"In other words, you don't trust me."

"We ain't sayin' we do and we ain't sayin' we don't," the warted man said. "All we're sayin' is that he's our friend and we'll see that he gets home all right."

Fargo came up to stand next to her.

McCarey looked embarrassed. "This ain't nothin' against you, Mr. Fargo. But my friends decided—"

"—his friends decided," Noelle said, "that I'm responsible for those other two men being robbed and killed. And that if you guard him tonight, the same thing will happen to him."

Her facade of strength slipped some. There was pain and vulnerability in her voice. "I don't want to see any of you boys in here ever again. Understand?"

The men were intimidated by her new tone. If she'd been angry with them, they could have been angry right back. But this was different. They'd hurt her and they knew they'd hurt her and this wasn't fair. This was how women fought you—with hurt feelings—and it just wasn't fair.

They let their heads hang. They couldn't look at her.

"It's nothin' personal," McCarey said, his voice weak.

Noelle turned away from them and headed to the bar.

Fargo stayed there. He decided to challenge them the way they'd challenged Noelle. "You sure you can trust these boys, McCarey?"

"Hey, what the hell's that supposed to mean?" the warted man said.

"I was talking to McCarey."

"Yeah, but we know what you meant."

"You sure you can trust them, McCarey?"

Some kind of silent signal must have passed between

the men. Because Fargo had barely spoken the words when the warted one lunged at him, and two of his cronies grabbed Fargo from either side.

"Nobody calls me a killer," the warted man said. And started proving his point by slamming three punches deep into Fargo's stomach.

Fargo was glad he hadn't eaten a lot. Otherwise he would have been awful queasy about now. Warts here knew how to throw a pretty good punch.

Fargo was ready for the fourth punch. Just as Warts was pulling back his fist to make sure the punch was delivered clean and hard, Fargo got the tip of his right foot ready. He made a connection as soon as Warts got close enough.

Warts leaned into his punch and that was when he got it. The old toe-in-the-nuts trick. Nothing new, nothing fancy, not Fargo's favorite tactic, but almost always reliable when you were outnumbered. Warts made a huge, ugly face—one even uglier than his regular face—and then sank slowly, clutching his crotch, to the floor.

A couple of things happened in this moment. Warts let out a scream that woke up people all over Oregon Territory. And Fargo took this precise second—when they were distracted by their friend's sudden misery—to whip his body free of human bonds.

He smashed the nose of his first captor. Blood sprayed everywhere. Then he took the man's arm and flung him hard against the wall. The man looked as if he was doing a vaudeville routine. He hit the wall, bounced off and then fell over backwards, the back of his head cracking against the floor.

The second captor was luckier. All Fargo did to him was smash him in the right eye, deliver a short chop to his throat, drive a fist deep into his sternum and then pound his head a few times against a table. The man had the good sense to slide into a chair before he passed out.

But just as he was deciding who to start in on next, Noelle took his arm and said, "C'mon, let me buy you a drink."

"I'm real sorry about this," McCarey said. "It really ain't nothin' personal. The boys just want to protect me."

Noelle nodded to the three men on the floor. "Yes, and they look like they're doing a real good job of it, too, Rufe."

They went to the bar. Fargo drank beer. Noelle said, "All the years I've put into this place and they don't even trust me. I run a clean operation here, Skye."

"Well, you did all you could. If something happens to McCarey, you're not responsible."

"But they'll think I am. And that's the trouble." She touched long, elegant fingers to her temple. "I'm getting one of my headaches. Sometimes they get so bad I have to stay in bed for a couple of days. I've learned to head off the worst of it by going to bed right away. If there's anything you need, just ask Sam." She touched his arm. "I'll see you tomorrow, I hope."

"I'll be here," Fargo said.

They both laughed. She stood on tiptoe and kissed him good night.

He spent the next few minutes relaxing. Sleep sounded good. A good mattress, clean sheets, a heavy blanket. Sounded damned good.

He'd just turned down the bartender's offer of another beer when he heard somebody behind him say, "I guess I've changed my mind, Mister Fargo. I'd appreciate it if you'd ride home with me." Rufe McCarey stepped up to the bar. "If that's still all right, I mean."

5

They abused him and he paid them back, Philly did. They laughed at him and scorned him and kicked him in the pants and even spit on him. But Philly always paid them back in some way.

Not that they knew that he paid them back. To look at the shaggy, odiferous form of Philly, you wouldn't think he had any skills. A man with skills wouldn't allow himself to look, act, or stink this way. A man with skills—even the merest skills—would sober himself up and get himself a job and make a life for himself.

But that was all behind Philly now and had been for a long time. Oh, he'd do a little work—swamp a saloon out; unload a wagon here and there; wash windows from time to time—when he needed to, if that was the only way he could get himself a drink. But most of the time he'd just wheedle, mooch, and plead for a drink, and most people got so sick of seeing him—let alone listening to him—that they'd give him the price of a pint of rotgut just to get rid of him.

Every once in awhile, though, he'd use his skills, which came in the form of tiny burglary tools he'd taken off a dead hobo several years back. The flies and the crows were a-picking at the man by the time Philly got to him, but that was all right. The flies and the crows weren't interested in the tools. And thank God because those tools had saved Philly from the hell of sobriety many times.

Tonight, he put his skill in practice for two reasons. He needed some money for alcohol. And he wanted to thumb his nose at a leading citizen by breaking into his place of business and stealing the price of a pint. The leading citizen had pontifically insulted him yesterday.

The leading citizen ran one of those places that stayed open late. What Philly had to do was wait until everybody inside got distracted up front. Then Philly would use his tools to get into the back door. And make his way to the leading citizen's office. Philly had been inside many times and knew just where everything was.

It took an hour before he got his chance, all this time waiting out in the chilly, coarse wind, in the darkness, listening to the human noises inside, everything from laughter to rage. Then he crept up to the back door and let himself in.

He had to work fast, he knew. Had to work fast and clear out fast. Because the leading citizen's office was way up front and you never knew when one of the employees might have to go in the back. And there Philly'd be. Stealing. And wouldn't the town just love that. The scorn would be unbearable then. And Philly would be forced to leave. And where would he go? He had no illusions about himself. Who would want him? He pictured the dead hobo he'd taken the burglary tools from. He'd be that hobo. He pictured himself lying next to the railroad tracks, the flies and the crows having at him the way they had at the hobo.

No . . .

He slipped inside.

A lot of loud human noise up front.

He moved close to the wall of the corridor, glad that there wasn't any direct lantern light back here at this time of night. He tried to become one with the shadows.

The office door was closed. What if he had to take the time to unlock it? Working outside was an advantage. Nobody heard you. But inside—

The door was unlocked. He hurried inside.

Faint moonlight revealed an orderly office that smelled of ink, tobacco, and furniture polish.

He went straight to work. Most people in this man's position kept cash of some kind in their desk drawers. Philly searched through four such drawers before finding what he wanted. An envelope with *Petty Cash* written on the outside of it. There were six greenbacks inside. Philly took three, and stuffed them in his pocket.

He was just about to get up out of his crouch when he decided he needed to check the very last drawer on the left bottom of the desk.

And that was where he found them. Two photographs, three letters. He couldn't help himself. Curious, he took them to the window. He was not immediately aware of their significance.

Suddenly he heard footsteps and a voice trailing its way back to the office. Somebody was coming. Somebody was definitely coming.

He quickly returned the photographs and the letters. And then he saw that the office door was open a half inch. He hadn't closed it tight, apparently.

He hunched down behind the desk as the footsteps in the hall grew closer.

The steps stopped abruptly. Whoever it was had apparently found the door ajar. The door squeaked as the man pushed it open. "Hello? Anybody in here?" he called.

The murky light from the hall cut a line through the gloom of the office. Philly thought he was going to be sick. He'd been caught at last. The man took a few more steps into the office and said aloud to himself, "This is supposed to be closed." He took a few more steps. Philly wished he could shrink down to the size of a kitten.

Then the visitor grunted a few words to himself and closed the door the way Philly should have.

Philly had to wait until the man went to the back, did whatever he wanted to, and walked up front again. Philly then made his escape.

It was not until he was three blocks away that Philly realized what he'd seen in those photographs and letters. And then suddenly he knew who was killing Noelle Caine's customers.

Philly smiled to himself. No more breaking into places, risking hide and hair for a little liquor money. Oh, no. Philly had stumbled upon a brand-new source of cash. A lot of cash. And a regular stream of it.

*   *   *

43

After the rain, the air was clean and cool and made Fargo wish he was in bed. The stage road was muddy after all the rain. On both sides of the road there were timberland, gorges, and ravines.

"This is probably a pretty nice road when it's dry," Fargo said.

"It is. It's a lifesaver in the winter, Trailsman."

"Listen, how about just calling me Fargo. That Trailsman thing—"

"Oh, yeah. I forgot you asked me about that." He expectorated with such size and volume, Fargo half-expected a tree to fall over. "I'll just call you Trailsman when I'm tellin' my grandkids about tonight."

"That sounds fair."

So they rode on, a crisp, perfect night of full moon and wind-tossed autumn trees and hawks crying as they swept down the air currents. They both stopped to piss at one point. And then McCarey said, once they were riding again, "You're a friend of Noelle's, huh?"

"Never laid eyes on her till tonight."

"Well, I'd sure like to lay more than my eyes on her."

"You don't really think she killed those two men, do you?"

"A lot of people think she shot her sister. So what would stop her from killin' those men?"

"I met her husband," Fargo said. "Hard to believe that two smart, good-looking women would fight over a fancy boy like him."

"They lined up in this town," McCarey said, "the ladies, I mean. And accordin' to everything I heard, he did 'em up nice and fine. And they kept comin' back for more, too."

Fargo shook his head. Sometimes women acted almost as crazy as men. Almost.

The roar—though it was only partly a roar, the other part being something like a scream—cleaved the night with its fury. Both men had to hold the reins tight to steady their horses. Deep rustling sounds in the forest told Fargo that many night creatures were shifting positions—finding better places to hide—to avoid the beast that had just roared.

"Puma," Fargo said.

"His name's Goldie."

Fargo laughed. "He sounds like he could eat the whole Territory in one mouthful—and you call him Goldie?"

"Well, if you'd ever seen him, you'd see why. He looks like somebody painted him with gold. He's one beautiful cat. And some of the ranchers turned him into a deadly one, too."

"What happened?"

"Oh, a few of their livestock got picked off by some wolves. So they started killin' every wolf they could find. And by the time they'd drove off the wolves, they decided to keep goin' and kill off the pumas, too. Around here, we call 'em mountain lions, but they're the same thing."

"Goldie's one of the few left?"

"Maybe the only one. Their excuse was they were afraid that the pumas would start attacking human beings."

"But pumas don't usually bother human beings."

"Try tellin' that to a bunch of know-nothin' ranchers who just want to have themselves a good time shootin' everything that moves. Anyway, they shot enough pumas so that Goldie finally did start attackin' human beings. There's a $500 reward out for killin' him."

The puma screamed again, and to Fargo the pitch of the noise seemed to lend the shadowy landscape an alien look as if he'd been transported to some other world. The ravines and gorges looked deeper and even deadlier now. And the forest took on aspects of the haunted ones children were always warned about in fairy tales.

"How far to your place?" Fargo now asked Rufe.

"Little over a mile or so. We crest that hill up there, you'll be able to see my little place down in the valley. I'm gonna buy my wife some real nice things to fix the house up with. She's been waitin' a long time for some of the little extras."

Fargo enjoyed listening to the Scotsman talk about his wife. The man not only loved her, but liked her and appreciated all the things she'd brought to his life. He didn't stay in town to drink and go whoring with the money. He took it straight home to his family.

If Fargo had glanced to the north just then, he would have seen the silhouette of a person behind a large, rough-surfaced boulder lean out from the hiding place and aim a Winchester directly at where Fargo would be in half a minute. Thirty seconds would give the shooter plenty of time to get set for the shot.

The sound of the two quick shots clapped and thundered across the hill of buffalo grass that Fargo and McCarey had just started to climb.

Their horses bucked. McCarey, who'd been riding slightly ahead of Fargo, turned to see a bullet tear into the edge of Fargo's skull, igniting an explosion of blood and bone fragments that formed a fan against the stark circle of moon. It was not without a certain ghoulish beauty.

McCarey turned his horse, wanting to ride back and help Fargo—

Fargo felt pain. Rushing darkness. A sense of falling, falling.

Fargo tried to collect himself in the panic and frenzy of the moment.

I've been shot, he thought. *Am I going to die?*

Falling. Crashing. The pain grew even more intense. More intense . . .

Darkness complete now. A collision of thoughts, memories, instincts . . .

And then Fargo slipped into utter oblivion, completely unaware of everything going on around him . . .

And came out on the other side . . .

Above him Fargo saw the fiery autumnal trees ignited by moonlight. Massive thunderheads were collecting. A wind that smelled and tasted of mountain winters was blowing.

His entire body was shivering. A fury of pain on the side of his head. The stench and feel of blood congealed on the side of his face.

He sat up carefully, trying to minimize the pounding pain that half-paralyzed him. He managed to crawl slowly to his knees. He wavered there. His vision was terrible, as if somebody had smeared grease over his eyes. He had to squint to bring anything into focus. And the squinting only made his head hurt more.

He saw the horse first. The paint that McCarey had
been riding. The animal was sprawled statue-like in the
buffalo grass. Not even the fierce wind could move such
a huge dead thing.

And where was McCarey?

6

Fargo wondered how long he'd been unconscious. Long enough for the horse to be killed. Long enough for McCarey—

He saw the small man, then. Face down in a small clear patch. As still as his horse. Fargo forced himself to his feet, staggering in the vicinity of the dead man. Twice, he fell to his knees. The second time, he wondered if he could ever get back up again.

What had happened? Who had done this?

He reached for his Colt. Maybe the killer was still around. He had to have his Colt . . .

But his holster was empty. Where was his Colt?

He stumbled forward to McCarey, remembering the money now, remembering the robbed and dead men now, remembering that he'd agree to ride with McCarey to protect him. And now McCarey was dead.

Fargo eased himself to his knees. Turned McCarey over.

A gauzy moment—a moment of unreality—some plane of existence not his own—McCarey staring up at him with the eyes of death, blood smeared all over his face. Staring at him as the wind shrieked. Staring at him as a crow cried. Staring at him as the stink of McCarey's bowels filled Fargo's nostrils.

Fargo had seen a lot of dying and death in his time and was not easily touched by it. You see enough of it, you grow hardened by it. But not tonight. Not this little Scotsman taking his winnings home to his sweet little wife.

He brought his head up slightly at a nearby sound. But his vision was so fuzzy, he couldn't be sure that he was seeing—a boy? A young boy near the edge of the forest, looking at him? But what would a young boy be doing out here now? He had to be imagining things. Had to be.

They'd been riding along and everything had been fine and now—

When he pitched forward, he landed but a few feet from McCarey. And there he lay for the next few hours, his breathing troubled, his heart beating out a rough and uncertain rhythm, his unconscious mind an unending corridor of nightmarish screams and images.

Sick, he was sick. Dying, he was dying.

He did not hear the three men who came sometime later, riding hard as they scanned the buffalo grass. A big man with a full black beard going gray and a black patch on his right eye rode a roan. He carried a Sharps in his left hand and his reins in the other. On the left front of his sheepskin glistened a sheriff's star.

The other two men were younger. They, too, wore badges, but they also wore the callow expressions of uncertainty. They had been deputized as part of a posse, first time they'd ever worn stars, both fearing not the man they were searching for but the man they were riding with. Sheriff Tom Bradshaw liked to say he had killed somewhere between thirty and forty men, he just wasn't sure of the exact number. Now some lawmen when they said things like that, you knew they were bullshitting you. Not Tom Bradshaw. You knew he was telling you the truth. The two young men were wise to be intimidated by this man.

They didn't have any trouble finding McCarey and Fargo. The buffalo grass wasn't taller than the shank of the average horse so hiding out in it was impossible. They spent less than ten minutes searching this plateau.

One of the young men saw the dead horse first. He spurred his animal over for a closer look and then let loose an excited shout. Bradshaw and the other deputy hurried over to see what had so excited the young man.

Bradshaw ground-tied his horse. He took his Sharps with him. Then he went over and stood above Rufe

McCarey's body. "Sonofabitch," he said. "I'll be the one who has to tell Josie McCarey, won't I? Me'n Rufe's been friends for better than twenty years."

The young men knew he was talking to himself.

"Dammit, Rufe," Bradshaw said, "why couldn't you stay home where you belonged? You go out to those damned casinos, you're just askin' for trouble."

The young men were silent. They knew he was still talking to himself.

Bradshaw stared down at Rufe a while longer and then walked over to the other man.

"You can see his breath," one of the young men said.

"He's still alive," said the other.

Bradshaw looked at the men. "He faked this whole thing. Soon as I heard the deal him and Noelle cooked up, I knew this was gonna happen. He'd make it look like somebody shot at them and made off with Rufe's money."

Bradshaw rammed the barrel of his Sharps hard against Fargo's head wound. "I ought to finish this bastard off right here and now."

The two young men gaped at each other. Tom Bradshaw was even scarier than they'd heard.

"Right here and now," Bradshaw said.

Then he knelt down and handcuffed Fargo's wrists behind his back.

He came to smelling some of the harsh-scented medicines familiar to frontier doctors' offices. Fargo had to orient himself, reconstruct everything that had happened this evening. The Ruby Rooster, Rufe McCarey, the ambush, the astonishing pain in his head—

Doctor Givens was a tall, swarthy man with pure-white hair and vivid-blue eyes that held the same irony as his mouth. Given all the dying and death he'd seen, he probably needed a strong dose of irony to get through his days. The damnedest things happened to people, and if you didn't laugh at them sometimes, you couldn't survive in his particular calling.

He said, "You're a lucky man, Fargo."

"So I've been told."

"If that bullet had cut upward or moved a quarter

inch to the right, we wouldn't be having this conversation. You'd be sportin' a pair of wings."

"Or a pitchfork."

Givens smiled with gleaming store-boughts. "I kind've suspected that but I didn't want to say it."

"What happened?"

"Somebody shot you."

"Thanks for the information," Fargo said sarcastically. "I meant, how did I get here?"

"Bradshaw brought you in. He wants me to fix you up so he can hang you."

"Hang me? For what?"

Fargo lay on an examination table. Only when he tried to sit up did his head hurt. It hurt with blinding pain. "I guess I'm not as tough as I thought," he said.

"Nobody is," the old doctor said. "As for why he wants to hang you, he thinks you killed Rufe McCarey."

"Rufe is dead?"

"I'm afraid so. I got the body in back waitin' for the funeral home wagon."

Despite the pain, Fargo forced himself to sit up. "I must've been out for a long time."

Doctor Givens nodded. "You looked a lot worse than you felt. But I'm serious about Bradshaw. He said to patch you up so he could take you to jail."

"I didn't kill anybody."

"I didn't figure you did. Bradshaw's judgment isn't for shit. But he's got folks around here convinced that he knows what he's doin'. I'll tell you what, when he comes burstin' in here, what you do is just lay there and we'll pretend like you're unconscious."

"How come you're helping me?" Fargo said.

"I'm not helping you. I'm helping myself. Gives me a lot of pleasure to run Bradshaw around in circles. I get tired of seein' him strut around this town likes he's lord and master."

"So I just lay here and—"

Doctor Givens said, "Son, it ain't real hard to play a corpse. Now shut up and lay down there. I think I hear him on the front porch."

Givens was right. It sounded as if his home office was being invaded by a herd of mean-meaning animals.

Fargo had always thought of trying a little acting, anyway. Givens was right. How hard could it be to play a corpse?

Ever since she'd been shot, Fiona Caine had had trouble sleeping. She was frequently awake when Noelle came home late from the casino. She generally read the novels of the day. She always told people that she was especially fond of the books in which courageous heroines went around the world having tremendous adventures. People always nodded pityingly when she told them that. Poor thing. She can't walk. Or run. Or swim. But she can read about young women who can do all those things. The poor, sweet thing. Cut down like that. And they've never found out who shot her, either. The poor thing.

Tonight's book was about a hero rather than a heroine, Sir Walter Scott's *Ivanhoe*. She loved the colorfulness of Scott's novels, the legend and lore of castles and dungeons and maidens swooning over handsome heroes.

She sat next to the fireplace, warmed by her tea and her blanket, absorbed in her book. She scarcely heard Noelle come in. Noelle smelled of night and rain. As she was hanging her rain cape in the vestibule, she said, "Rufe McCarey was killed tonight."

"He didn't—?"

"Oh, but he did," Noelle said, coming into the living room. She went over to the fire and warmed her hands. "He won a lot of money, and then when he was on the way home somebody robbed and killed him. I even sent a man along named Skye Fargo to protect him."

"Skye Fargo? I met him tonight." Fiona tapped her novel. "He's sort of a Western version of a Sir Walter Scott hero."

"He's not in very good shape right now, I'm afraid," Noelle said. "Whoever ambushed Rufe ambushed Fargo, too."

"Oh, my Lord—he's not going to die, is he?"

Noelle smiled. "I see he got to you."

Fiona waved a dismissive hand. "You're being silly. I just liked him is all."

Noelle laughed. "I like him, too. Especially those tight-fitting buckskins he wears."

Fiona had to laugh, too. "You're shameless sometimes, Noelle. You really are."

"So are you, sister dear, you just won't admit it. That's the one big difference between us, Fiona."

Noelle carried Fiona's teacup to the kitchen, where she warmed it with hot water from the still-steaming pot. As she walked out of the living room, she felt Fiona's envious eyes on her. She knew two truths about this situation, Noelle did—one being that if she were in Fiona's situation, she too would be jealous of Noelle. And truth number two—that Fiona still suspected that Noelle had shot her in the back and paralyzed her because she was jealous and angry about Rick. Just beneath the surface of all this sisterly fondness, Fiona felt great rage and hatred for her sister. Noelle was sure of it.

When she returned with the tea, Noelle said, "I see Philly was here this afternoon again. I really worry about you being alone with him."

"He's harmless."

"I wonder," Noelle said.

"He tells me things," Fiona said. She smiled. "Secrets."

Noelle said coldly, "Maybe he'll tell you who shot you."

Fiona was equally icy. "Maybe he already has, Noelle. Maybe he's already told me that it was somebody very, very close to me."

"That's not very amusing."

"It wasn't meant to be," Fiona said.

Noelle turned from the table where she'd set her sister's tea and marched quickly to the stairs. She paused on the second step and said, "Remind me not to be so damned nice to you all the time."

7

He'd slept eight hours in Doctor Given's office and had then been brought over here to the jail in handcuffs and leg shackles. Bradshaw had made sure to take the most public route. They'd been trailed by a small group of kids who kept yelling, "Are you a killer, mister?"

And Bradshaw obliged by saying, "He sure is. And we're gonna hang him, too."

"Can we watch?"

"Sure you can. Does a kid good to see justice in action."

Fargo had spent his share of time in jail. Some were a lot better than others. In Mexico, if you had the money, they let you have "conjugal" visits with prostitutes. Now, there was a truly enlightened country. This jail wasn't as bad as you might have expected, given Bradshaw's personality. It was clean, the guard was amiable enough, and Bradshaw made only one appearance in three hours. He came to the cell to tell Fargo, "Your lawyer Withers'll be here pretty soon. I already know what happened. But we have to go through the motions. You'll have twenty minutes."

"That's very nice of you, Sheriff," Fargo said. "But I'm sure I can wrap it up faster than that." He beamed at Bradshaw. "All I need to tell him is that I didn't kill Rufe."

Bradshaw said, "Just about every man I send to the gallows tells me he's innocent. Nice to know you ain't gonna be any different."

* * *

Prescott G. Withers showed up half an hour later. For an old fart with some kind of rash on his face, he looked absolutely dapper and chipper. "You have just gotten some very good news, my friend," he intoned, in a voice that had thrilled juries in every courtroom in the Territory.

Fargo touched his temple. "Somebody's going to get me a new head?"

"Even better than that. You're a free man."

Fargo raised his hands with the clattering shackles. "No more of these?"

"No more of those. And no more of Tom Bradshaw's badgering you, either."

"What the hell happened?"

Prescott G. Withers stepped into the cell and said, "Rufe's son, Tom—he's eleven—was out chasing a pony that had run away. He saw everything from the woods—saw his father killed, and you shot by a sniper. He came into town with his mother this morning and told Bradshaw everything. Bradshaw refused to believe any of it so they went to old Judge Forsythe. And when the judge heard I was handling the case, he told me what the McCareys told him."

"That also means whoever killed Rufe—and tried to kill me—is still on the loose."

For the first time, the crusty old lawyer, prim, proper, a bony hand hanging off the lapel of his suitcoat, looked unhappy. "I hear in your voice the sound of a man who wants vengeance."

"Wouldn't you want vengeance?"

"Maybe in some other town. But not in Cumberland."

"Oh? And why not?"

"Because Tom Bradshaw didn't like you on general principle even before you came to town. He hates people who get written up in the newspapers more than he does. But now he's got a specific reason. He spent eighteen hours going around town bragging about how he'd caught Rufe's murderer and how he was going to hang you. Then Tom McCarey and his mother come to town and spoil everything. Now he looks like a fool—or thinks he does, which is the same difference. And he thinks you're the one who made him look like a fool."

Withers helped Fargo unshackle himself. Fargo was still unsteady. "Now you can get on your horse and ride on out of town, Fargo."

"I'm not sure I'm going to do that."

"Noelle was hoping you'd say that."

"You know Noelle?"

"I should. She's my niece. My late wife and I raised her and her sister."

"Is it true that Noelle's husband came between her and Fiona?"

"That's a subject I don't care to talk about. With anybody. Never have, never will."

"So you don't have an opinion if Noelle shot Fiona."

"Of course I have an opinion, Fargo. But it's a privately held opinion. I have a lot of opinions that are privately held. That's how I've lived to be seventy-three and have a reasonably prosperous life. I'm not always handing out my opinions. That's the fastest way I know to make enemies."

"Bradshaw doesn't seem to think much of Noelle."

Withers snorted. "Bradshaw doesn't think of anybody except Bradshaw."

"I kind've got that impression."

"Noelle herself would ride out of here if she could, Fargo."

"What's stopping her?" Fargo said.

"What's stopping her? What do you think is stopping her? Fiona. She takes care of her sister."

"She does?"

"Sure. She has a room right down the hall from Fiona's She even sleeps there part of the time, when she doesn't sleep at the casino. She loves her sister more than anybody else in the world."

"She still might have shot her," Fargo said.

"You're a very cynical man, Mr. Fargo."

"So are you."

"True, but I wasn't cynical when I was your age. It took me a lot longer to lose my innocence." Withers walked to the door of the cell. "Well, good-bye, Mr. Fargo. For your sake I hope I never see you again."

An hour later, Fargo sat in a café eating a plate of

eggs, ham, fried potatoes and hominy grits. This was going to be a four-cup-of-coffee breakfast. He needed the lift and the nervous energy.

Nearly everybody who came into the place paused a moment to gawk at him. He had become a celebrity. Bradshaw had probably convinced at least half of them that Fargo was a killer, despite what Tom McCarey said.

Fargo was just starting on his third cup of coffee when Rick Kingsley, Noelle's estranged husband, came in.

He was, as always, fast on the draw with a smirk. He was dressed in different colors but the same style, a dove-gray riverboat gambler's suit with a blue brocade vest, white ruffled shirt, and a string tie with a blue catch at the top. He came over and sat down uninvited. "Well, I guess congratulations are in order," he said.

"I guess I don't remember asking for company," Fargo replied.

"I guess I shouldn't have expected you to have good manners. A man who'd sleep with another man's wife can't be counted on to be very civilized."

"If you're trying to make me feel guilty, you can forget it, Kingsley. She hasn't been your wife in a long time, not since you started sleeping with her sister."

"Things happen, Fargo."

"So I hear."

"Things happen, and afterward all we can do is regret them."

Fargo stared at him. "So you regret having an affair with Fiona?" he asked

The smirk became a grin. "Now, I didn't say that. Fiona is even more inventive in bed than dear Noelle."

"Yeah," Fargo said, "especially now that she's crippled from the waist down."

Kingsley gave a little jerk of surprise. "You can be a very harsh man, Fargo."

"What is it you want exactly, Kingsley?"

"Believe it or not, I want to hire you."

"No, thanks."

"You don't even want to know why I want to hire you?"

"No."

The smirk again. "Well, I'm going to tell you, anyway.

I want you to save Noelle's reputation. I've been a terrible husband—I admit it—and I hurt her very deeply. And I want to try and make it right."

"What brought this on?"

"You. And the way people talked about you and Noelle after Rufe McCarey was killed. They said that you'd conspired together to kill him. That implied that my wife was a cold-blooded killer. She isn't. She's an honest, decent, thoughtful woman."

"If she's such a good woman, why'd you treat her the way you did?"

Kingsley sighed. "I told you. Things happen. I'm not an angel. I'm certainly not going to try and tell you that. But I didn't go around deliberately trying to betray my wife, either. It just—happened—with Fiona. I'm sure you've done things you're ashamed of, Fargo."

Fargo remembered Kingsley's grin of a few moments ago. He hadn't seemed ashamed of what he'd done at all. Which was the real Rick Kingsley—the cad or the remorseful husband? Maybe a little bit of both. That was one of the troubles with human beings, Fargo had noted long ago. They were never easy to figure out. And sometimes they didn't even know themselves when they were telling the truth.

"The answer is still 'no.'"

"You're dooming her to one hell of a life, Fargo."

"Meaning what?"

"Meaning because Fiona won't move, Noelle has to stay here. And be distrusted and despised by practically everybody in this town. You really want that for her? If you could find the real killer—and he's now killed three people, counting Rufe—she could at least stay here and not have this cloud over her."

"Bradshaw can't find out?" Fargo queried.

"Bradshaw's a gunny, not a detective," Kingsley said.

Fargo still didn't believe the man's story. Just want to help the little lady out, Fargo. Bullshit. But since Fargo had decided to look for the killer himself, he might as well pretend to be helping out Kingsley, here. Maybe that way he'd find out what Kingsley was really up to.

Fargo sighed. "All right. For Noelle's sake."

Kingsley's face reflected his obvious surprise. "That was quick—changing your mind."

"Bradshaw wants me out of town fast. I wonder why. I might as well look for the killer while I'm staying here, to annoy Bradshaw."

"He going to come after you, Fargo."

"I'm looking forward to it."

The smirk. "You're a cocky bastard. Don't let his white hair fool you. He's got enough mean in him for ten men your age. You should see him beat a confession out of somebody sometime. It'd make you sick to your stomach. He damn near killed a friend of mine that way."

Kingsley stood up. Shoved his hand forward. For a moment, Fargo thought about not shaking. But what the hell. It was a meaningless gesture, anyway. He shook hands.

The deputy started tailing him about half a block from the café. Fargo would have led him a merry chase if he wasn't so damned exhausted by his head troubles.

The pharmacy was open. He went in and bought some things he'd been needing anyway—namely, headache powder and some ointment for a saddle burn on the edge of his right cheek—and then amused himself by glancing out the window every few minutes so the highly unskilled deputy would have to fling himself out of sight.

He went straight to his hotel room and stripped down to his underwear and slid beneath the covers and went to sleep. He was in dreamland—good dreams, wine, women, and more women—when a reluctant knock was knuckled against his door.

He reached down to the floor next to his bed and picked up his Colt, which was lying there naked. He pointed it at the center of the door and said, "Who is it?"

"My name's Bowen, Mister Fargo. I'm a friend of Philly's."

"Who?"

"Philly. You was gonna help him the other night. You found him in the street."

The town drunk, Fargo remembered. "What about him?"

"I'm scared for him."

"Come back tomorrow."

"He's doin' somethin' real foolish, Mister Fargo."

Leather-soled steps in the hall. Then rattle of silver coins in pockets. A couple of drummers laughing drunkenly as they headed for their rooms. A light, cold rain against the window. Fargo needed to piss and his head hurt. And he was talking to somebody he didn't know or trust, through a door. Somebody who could easily have been sent by Bradshaw.

"Tomorrow," Fargo said.

"He may not be around tomorrow, if you know what I mean." Bowen spoke in a loud whisper.

"Aw, shit," Fargo said, throwing the blankets back and his feet off the bed.

He stormed through the shadows to the door and flung it open. The little man with the leprechaun face and the derby hat was a ridiculous figure. If he'd bathed since the time Columbus had come rolling across the sea—the stink of whiskey and filth was powerful—Fargo would have been surprised. He had big sad eyes like a sick dog's, and a twitch in his right hand that could have been anything from palsy to liquor problems. In his case, it was obvious which one he suffered from.

"What the hell do you want?" Fargo demanded.

"It's Philly, Mister Fargo. I think he knows who killed McCarey and them other two men."

8

"He didn't tell you who he thinks the killer is?" Fargo asked.

"No, sir. He just said that whoever it is is gonna give him a lot of money."

"When was the last time you saw him?"

"This morning. He was just soberin' up. Sleepin' down by the trestle bridge where we all sleep sometimes. He was braggin' about it. About the money he was gonna get, I mean."

"And you didn't get any sense whatsoever of who he might have been talking about?"

"Nope. Afraid I didn't."

"So why did you come to me?"

"Because he's my friend. And because I'm scared for him."

The elfin man sat on the very edge of the hardback chair. He had a tic in his right eye and he kept belching sourly as he spoke.

"You think the man he's blackmailing will kill him?"

"Sure. People like us, we just don't luck into money like that. There's always a price. And you start blackmailin' people—"

Fargo was fully awake now. He had to agree with Bowen here. Even if Philly did know who the real killer was, it was unlikely the man being blackmailed would come through with the big payment.

"I heard all over town that Philly got all cleaned up and dried out and is wearin' new duds," Bowen said. "I looked for him but couldn't find him."

"So the man must've given Philly a little money in advance."

"That's what I was thinkin'."

"If you wanted to start looking for Philly, where would you go?"

"That's the thing. If it was the old Philly, I'd know exactly where to look. But if Philly's got some money—" He shrugged.

"I want to find Philly, too."

"I figured you would. That's why I came up here."

"How you fixed for money, Bowen?"

The leprechaun smiled with nubby brown teeth even more vile than Philly's. "Now how you think I'm fixed for money, Mister Fargo?"

"I need your help with this. You take all the places Philly would go if he was on the bottle. I'll take the more respectable places."

"You said somethin' about money, Mister Fargo."

Fargo reached up on the bureau. Bowen had been eyeing a stack of greenbacks Fargo had sitting there. He handed Bowen a couple of bills. "Buy yourself a good meal. Then start looking for Philly. I'm going to start tonight. Why don't we meet up later. Maybe one of us'll have some luck."

So much for the good night's sleep Fargo had been planning to get tonight.

"I don't wanna see Philly die, Mister Fargo," Bowen said, stuffing the relatively clean money into a smudgy pocket of his filthy trousers.

"I don't, either," Fargo assured him.

"But I don't want to see him die because he's my friend. You only care about him because he can tell you who the killer is."

Fargo said, "The world's like that sometimes, Bowen. I don't like it that way, but there isn't much I can do about it. Now get your ass going. I'll see you in three hours."

Bowen walked to the door. "You wouldn't think there'd be many places to hide in this town. But there are. And Philly knows every one."

Fargo said, "There's one thing I forgot to ask you."

"What?"

"Does Philly have a gun?"

"He didn't. But the same fella who said he saw Philly all duded up said he saw Philly comin' out of the gunsmith's with a brand new Colt."

"You think he knows how to use it?"

"He knows all he needs to know, Mister Fargo. If the man he's blackmailin' don't come across with all the money, all Philly has to do is point the gun at him and shoot. I'm scared of that, too. Philly don't always use his head."

"That's if," Fargo said, "the other man hasn't already shot Philly first."

Bowen's head jerked. "I guess I hadn't thought of that."

"I had," Fargo said. "In fact, that's the very first thing I did think of. People being blackmailed have been known to kill the people who shake them down. Philly better be damned careful with this man he's dealing with. Damned careful."

Bowen nodded somberly and left.

Fargo made the circuit of all the saloons, ending up at the Ruby Rooster. Nobody had seen Philly or, if they had, they weren't willing to share that information with Fargo.

Noelle came and sat down at a table with him. "Whiskey?"

"Better have coffee."

"You don't look so good, Fargo. You still need some rest."

"No time for rest now." He told her about Philly.

She shook her quite beautiful head. "He's playing a dangerous game."

"Bowen says he has a gun."

She laughed harshly. "Oh, my God. The idea of Philly with a gun."

"I need to find him."

"You need rest, too."

"Not till I find Philly. He may be on to something."

"It'd be nice and easy, wouldn't it, if he knew who the killer was and told us?"

She was called away soon after. A disgruntled gambler

claimed he'd been cheated. Fargo couldn't hear what she was saying but he saw the ragged gambler—a ranch hand by his looks—visibly relax as she continued to speak.

Sam Pines came over and sat down. "Buy you a drink?"

"No, thanks. This coffee's fine. I need to go anyway."

"I wanted to thank you again for the other night."

Sam was the croupier the Swede had held hostage.

"You might've done the same for me," Fargo said.

"Maybe," Sam said, "if I was feeling brave. Anyway, just wanted to thank you again."

"My pleasure."

Just as Sam got up, a drunken man staggered toward the player piano and said, "I wanna hear Suzanna play." Fargo recognized the man as Buck, the same man who'd made a scene the other night. He angrily took his drink and splashed it all over the wooden frame of the instrument.

The bouncer was on him instantly. Not rough. But forceful, taking Buck's glass from him. Forcing him over to a table where his friends were. Admonishing the man's friends to get him out of there before there was real trouble.

"Sad case," Sam said.

"Suzanna must've been very popular."

"You should've seen her. Buck there ain't the only one who carried a torch for her. A lot of fellas did. Buck just had it worse than the others is all."

"No chance she was murdered?"

Sam shrugged. "Don't think so. Think she just got sick of it all. Some of them do, you know. It ain't an easy life, no matter how it looks."

He said good-bye. He'd been on break. He went back to his gaming table.

Buck was struggling against the power of his friends. They were trying to push him out through the batwing doors. He kept hollering for Suzanna. It was the kind of scene played out too often in saloons, craziness tinged with sadness. He finished his coffee and went back to looking for Philly.

* * *

The heavy-set woman with the eye-patch rose to get the door shortly after the knocking started, "Yeah? It's late," she complained. Then she squinted closer at the dark figure on the wobbly wooden steps leading to her front door.

"What happened to your eye, Ruth Ellen?" Philly said.

She grinned. "Shit sake's, Philly. I didn't even recognize ya all shaved and duded up and—"

"What happened to yer eye?"

She shrugged dismissively. "Oh, cowhand likes to play rough sometimes. Pays me extra so I don't give a shit, long as he don't break nothin'. Anyway, he give me a black eye, see? And don't you know the damned thing goes and gets infected. So here I am with a black eye. So what the hell you doin' out here, anyways, Philly?"

"I got money, Ruth Ellen."

"You got money?" She let out a vast whiskey whoop that made the moon jump. She was a one-woman crib on the edge of town, Ruth Ellen Patterson. She wasn't supposed to be here. Whores were limited strictly to the casinos. But she paid Bradshaw enough that he didn't bother her. She didn't do a lot of business—there just wasn't a lot of call for a two-hundred-fifty-pound woman—but then she didn't need to. She had her little house and about thirty kitty cats (or pussies as her customers invariably and hilariously called them) and she had her food and that was about all she needed. She kept her privates scoured clean and her hair done up nice and high and pretty—and she wasn't all that bad-looking actually, given her weight—and so she did all right. "Now, where would you get money, Philly? You stick somebody up?"

Philly grinned. There was pride in that grin. "Somethin' like that. Anyways, I want to spend the night here." He said it in such a way that he knew she'd be tickled by it. Make her feel special. Make her feel important. Make her feel she maybe didn't weigh that much after all; make her think she was somebody and not just some prairie nobody the way she really was.

"The whole night?"

"The whole night."

"Well, I'm kinda flattered." And she actually sounded flattered. "You finally get your hands on a little money and you come to see Ruth Ellen. That's awful sweet, Philly."

So he let her think it was awful sweet. He didn't tell her the real reason. That in town—walking around—he'd begun to get the sense that somebody was following him. And that he needed a place to lay low for the night. And hell, he might as well have a little fun while he was laying low.

"So can I come in?"

"I'm gonna need to see your money first, Philly."

Philly was ready. He showed her a few greenbacks. She whistled. And adjusted her eye-patch. "This damned thing is hell to keep on straight, Philly, you know that?"

Philly and Ruth Ellen went inside.

Neither of them saw the shape behind the tree a hundred yards away. The shape that had followed Philly out there from town.

They'd gone and changed deputies on Fargo.

He was making his second swing through the four saloons looking for Philly when he realized that the new one was bigger and looked a whole lot meaner. No more tyros. Bradshaw was getting serious now. Fargo was tired of being tailed. Bradshaw had no legitimate reason for having anybody tail him.

Fargo decided to test the new deputy's brain power. He was almost disappointed. The new one might be bigger and meaner, but he sure wasn't any smarter.

Fargo walked down a street until he came to the opening of an alley. He pretended to start across the alley to the other side. Then he vanished into the alley's shadows.

The deputy came lumbering after him. He drew his gun, he broke into a trot, he broke a sweat, he had mean intentions—but he fell for a gag that was old back when Imperial Rome still ran the world.

All Fargo did was stick his foot out of the deep darkness and trip the dumb bastard. Ass over appetite the deputy went. He landed facedown, and so hard that his six-shooter went flying out of his hand.

Fargo had to give him his *cajones*. The deputy jumped up—and his jaw had to hurt like hell after landing on it—and started swinging wildly at Fargo.

Fargo was ready. Or thought he was.

The deputy hit him with a force and ferocity that rocked Fargo back so far that he smashed his head against the clapboard wall behind him. This man could hit. Fargo didn't need any more pain.

He kept on hitting. Fargo had underestimated him. He smashed his fists into Fargo's face, chest, and ribs, and then started the rotation all over again.

Fargo knew he was in a fight. He started picking up on the deputy's rhythms. There was always a heavy-breathing moment of hesitation before the guy threw a punch, as if he needed that moment to decide where to put his fist. Fargo started using this hesitation to his own advantage, reading the punch just as it was thrown, and getting out of the way before it could land, or land clean, anyway.

The deputy got the advantage back by yanking a bowie knife from a sheath on the left side of his belt. He lunged. A ballet star he would never be, this deputy. When he lunged, his entire body followed the motion, and he pitched headlong past Fargo.

Fargo took the opportunity to put three punches in the deputy's ribs and then blast him hard on the side of the head. The last blow knocked the man off balance. And just as he'd lost his gun, now he lost his knife.

But once more the deputy showed he had a nine-lives constitution. He somehow managed to turn around with great agile speed and slam a punch into Fargo's sternum that cracked Fargo's head against the wall once again. A few seconds of utter blackness made Fargo worry he might not be able to finish the deputy off, something he most devoutly desired at this point. The prick had managed to really piss him off.

Fargo put one right on the man's jaw and without hesitating put two more into his chest. He backed the deputy up a good four feet, pounding him every inch of the way. But yet again the deputy not only absorbed the punishment, he seemed to rally to it. He leaned in to deliver a right-handed uppercut that Fargo didn't expect at all. Fargo had the sense that the man had driven Fargo's eyeballs up into the top of his head.

This time it was Fargo backing up, moving in a semi-circle so that he could regain his breath and composure. His face was hot and slick with blood and sweat. So was the deputy's, who was obviously appreciative of the small break they'd taken from expending energy, something that was now in short supply for both of them.

The deputy came at him again. Fargo grabbed the man by his hair and smashed three fast punches directly into the deputy's nose. Bone shattered; blood sprayed. Fargo then shot four fast punches into the man's midsection and then went, without pause, back to the man's face two more times.

The deputy became a comic figure, his arms windmilling, his legs staggering, as he tried to decide where he should let his body drop. Apparently this was an important decision to the deputy. He could have just fallen in his tracks, but instead he wandered around a little, glancing here and there.

When he finally went, he went fast and hard, collapsing in a human puddle on the sandy surface of the alley. He moaned a little, he cursed a little, he coughed a little, and then he fell silent, a massive form in a leather vest a big silver star, corduroy trousers, and Texas boots, lying there in disgrace.

"Be sure and tell Bradshaw you did a good job," Fargo said, meaning what he said. "I'll tell him the same thing next time I see him."

His search for Philly was over for the night. He staggered back to his hotel. Drummers coming out of the hotel saloon watched the bloody-faced man work his way up the stairs with great and obvious effort. The man was frightening to see, something out of a nightmare.

One step at a time, Fargo traversed the stairs, almost falling backward a couple of times. It had been a long time since he'd been in a fight like that. That deputy had been damned good.

Fargo swung open his bedroom door, prepared for some much needed rest. As his tired eyes found themselves resting on the luscious curves of the naked blonde lying in his bed, he suspected there would be no rest for the weary.

"I came to make the bed," she purred. "I noticed it needed some warming up."

Fargo felt a stirring in his buckskins and decided he wasn't that tired after all.

9

By the time Fargo rode out of town, it was going on midmorning.

He decided after he woke to pay the good reverend a visit. Halfway to Amis's he noticed tracks on the side of the road, which were still muddy from last night's rain.

No mistaking those tracks. Puma. Fargo had long, wide feet, but these tracks were about as big as the ones he'd make. And they left just about as deep an impression in the mud, too. This had to be a damned big fella. Maybe as much as one hundred twenty, one hundred thirty pounds. Pumas this big were a real threat. Amis's place was on the other side of a steep and wide hill from McCarey's farm. The animal was undoubtedly "Goldie," the mountain lion everybody wanted to kill.

Reverend Amis's spread wasn't difficult to find. A wooden cross that must have been twenty feet tall had been built on the side of a piney hill. And below it, in a wide basin of flat farmland, sat a church of whitewashed adobe and a small house with a scattering of outbuildings.

The place reminded Fargo of some of the communes he'd seen throughout the West. A number of religious groups and fringe political groups had established what were much like little hamlets for believers to live in. Most of them started with great ideals—not unlike the ones that Nathaniel Hawthorne had known Back East—but then collapsed under that old bugaboo, the human condition.

From what Fargo had been able to see, socialism was

a great idea—on paper. But it never worked because it was a perfect cover for lazy people to hide out in—and after a time the hard-working folks just naturally came to resent the slackers. Then there were all the power plays. A whole passel of folks wanted to be the leader and that was always the beginning of the end.

GOD'S PLACE read a large sign nailed to a tree to the right of the road that led to the farmhouse. A border collie rushed out to greet Fargo and look him over. She must have liked what she saw because she stayed friendly, her tongue wagging the whole time. She wanted Fargo to pet her. Nice to know that at least the dog was friendly.

From the church wandered a young, towheaded boy, no older than fourteen. He wore a faded cotton shirt and dungarees rolled up several times. Even then, he tripped over them as he walked toward Fargo.

"My pa, he ain't here," the kid said. He had wide, gray eyes that were more animal-like than human. Disturbing. Accusing.

"No, huh?"

"My sister is, though."

"Then I guess I'll see her."

The kid shook his head obstinately. "You shouldn't ought to, though."

"Oh? Why's that?"

" 'Cause every time a man comes for her, she gets into trouble." He made a face and then intoned like a preacher: "Sin trouble. Trouble of the flesh."

Fargo would have laughed, except the kid was sort of spooky. "What's your name?"

"Michael."

"Well, Michael, how about going to tell your sister I'm here?"

"You got a sinful face, mister."

"So do you."

"Do not," Michael said angrily.

"Do too," Fargo said. "Now go get your sister for me."

"I'm gonna tell my pa you said I had a sinful face."

"You do that," Fargo said. "Right after you go and get your sister for me."

Michael watched Fargo over his shoulder all the way to the house.

Fargo ground-tied the stallion. A hawk glided on the air currents. A crow gleamed on its perch atop the roof of the house. Two tabby kittens tumbled and battled away on the frontage grass. The clean air smelled of pine and soft scudding winds.

And then from the front door of the cabinlike house came a girl who had been put on this planet for only one purpose—to relieve all otherwise sensible men of their good sense.

She was seventeen at least; more probably eighteen. Her long, reddish hair framed a face that was both impish and somber at the same time. She watched Fargo with eyes that hinted at sorrow but that glistened every few seconds with amusement. By now, she was long used to the staggering effect she had on men.

There was nothing sexy about her attire. She wore an ancient, frayed man's shirt and a pair of equally worn denims. But my oh my how those cast-off clothes clung to every part of her body, from her small but ripely shaped breasts to the breathtaking curves of her hips and thighs. She carried a basket full of wet laundry to a loosely strung clothesline and set it down. When she bent over that way, Fargo was treated to the sight of a bottom that belonged to the ages and should be kept in a museum in Paris, France.

She started hanging clothes, seeming to take no note of him. Then she said, her back to him, "The Reverend told me I'm not supposed to talk to strangers. I've still got welts on my back from the last time he caught me doing it. So I'm gonna pretend you're not here."

"I'm trying to pretend Michael's not here," Fargo said. The eerie little kid stood watching them from the front stoop of the house.

"He's kinda scary sometimes," she said. "Like he's possessed or something. He even spooks our dad sometimes."

"I can see why." Then: "I wonder if you'd answer some questions for me."

"I can't, mister. I'm sorry."

"Your dad?"

"My dad and—" She hesitated, nodding to the front stoop. "Michael. You have to be real careful around him." Then: "But if you were to ask me something and I was to start talking to myself afterward—I can't see how that's talking to a stranger, can you? I mean, what's the harm in talking to yourself?"

"Why are you so scared?"

"Because maybe he sent you. My dad, I mean."

"Sent me?"

"To tempt me."

"He did that?"

She kept pinning up wet clothes, moving down the line, as she spoke. "One time he sent a very handsome young man out here to tempt me. And believe me, I was tempted. I've got the devil in me but good. And I know it. But the boy was so nervous—and he kept looking around so much—I caught on that the Reverend was tempting me. So I kept hold of myself. I didn't let ole Satan get me that time."

"None of my business, but if you hate it here so much, why don't you just walk away?"

She didn't answer for a long time. Maybe she hadn't heard him. She just kept pinning up clothes. The smell of the wet laundry was good. There was a creek nearby. She probably spent the first part of the morning down there getting all the clothes clean.

"You're even better-looking than that boy the Reverend sent around to tempt me."

"I thank you for that, miss. But you didn't answer my question. Why don't you just walk away?"

Her head started to turn. Then she stopped herself at the last moment. She faced the laundry again. "He knows things about me."

"Things?"

"Things nobody else knows. Things that could get me in trouble if he was to tell anybody." She hesitated. "And I could tell you some things about him that could get him in some real serious trouble."

Michael said, "You better watch your mouth, sister. And maybe you better think of Suzanna and how she repented. You should repent, too."

Fargo was amazed that the kid had heard her words.

She'd spoken softly and there was considerable distance between the clothesline and the house.

"He must be able to read minds," Fargo said.

"He's possessed by the devil," she said. "You ever notice his eyes? Those aren't human eyes."

By this time, Michael had come down from the stoop. He gave them the full view of his odd, accusing stare. But he went wide of them, walking to the small barn, disappearing into the shadows of the interior.

She had gone back to hanging washing, turning her back on Fargo.

Michael came riding hard out of the barn, not looking at either his sister or Fargo. He rode a roan bareback. For someone of his size and age, he exerted great control over the animal. He went right down the same trail Fargo had taken to come here. He didn't once look back.

"He's supposed to go into town and get some things for my dad," the girl said, wiping her wet hands on her dungarees. "I'm Grace, by the way." She smiled. "I'll bet you've heard all kinds of things about me."

"I've heard some things about your dad, but not you."

"Well, my dad means well. He helps a lot of people. He really does. He can get kind of self-righteous sometimes. And once in a while he'll kind of go overboard a bit. But he's not a bad sort, really. He's had to raise both Michael and I. But I think he overdid it a little with Michael."

She finished hanging the laundry. "Now I need to go check on the kittens. We've got a new litter."

He walked next to her on the way to the barn. "He mentioned Suzanna. Did you know her?"

"She came to my dad for help. Michael's right about her. She really did repent her whole life. Michael tried to drive her off. He said she was a messenger from the devil. But Dad stood firm. He doesn't always with Michael. It's like Michael takes over his mind or something. Like with the whippings. Dad tries to stop him but—"

She exulted seeing the kittens and didn't finish her sentence. She knelt down next to the blanket she'd fixed in the hay for the large mama tabby and her infinitesimal tabby kittens that were all mewls and squinched-shut

eyes and gleaming little noses. Fargo smiled. It was a
sweet sight, the seven little ones pressed close to their
mother's sweat-and-milk wrinkled belly fur, the teats
vivid pink against the furry white.

She spent a moment with each kitten and then stood
up and came straight to him. "I don't expect you'd want
to see the loft, would you?"

"Is it a nice, safe loft? I wouldn't want to go any-
place dangerous."

She laughed. "Boy, do you have a line of sheep dip."

"It's just that I'm easily frightened."

She stared at the thing growing in his pants. "Yeah,
I'll bet you are."

There was enough hay in the loft to make a nice,
natural bed. She led the way up the ladder and as soon
as he stepped off it and on to the loft itself, she began
undoing her blouse. She wore no undergarments. Her
breasts were young, taut, not spectacular in size, though
certainly full and elegant in their pear-shape and the
fresh pinkness of her large nipples.

She held them up to him like the treasures they were.
"It's been a while since I let a man see me like this.
You can bet my dad wouldn't approve."

He found his throat and his senses clogged with lust.
"You like to touch them?"

"I'd like to do a lot more than touch them."

She smiled. "Be my guest, Mister Fargo."

He came to her. Lifted his right hand and reached out
his fingers to feel the shape of her upturned left breast.
A gasp stuck in his throat.

"My, my," he managed to say.

"You want to taste them?"

"Love to."

She took two steps forward. He bent down and began
licking them. She put a gentle hand on the back of his
head, guiding him from breast to breast with tender desire on her own part. He was hardly aware of her using
her free hand to shimmy her pants down. And then she
was guiding the fingers of his left hand inside of her. His
knees nearly buckled.

They sank to the hay. He parted her legs and began
to partake of her sex, his tongue knowing, sly, wise in

the ways of pleasuring a woman. She groaned, writhing as he moved deeper into her sweet darkness. He held her hands against her hips as she proceeded to have sex with him, his tongue a surrogate for his rod. Harder and harder she pushed against him, a frenzy of gasps, moans, muttered words he couldn't decipher.

He lost count of how many times she went past the brink. Eight or nine for sure. Then she raised her head and grinned down at him and said, "Don't worry about me. I've got plenty left to go."

It was her turn to work on him. She lay him back on the straw and began working him with both her tongue and mouth, concentrating at first on the tip so that she had him spellbound and out of control almost at once. She played with him until he was bucking like a bronc; and then she would stop and begin licking the ever-growing length of him.

She obviously enjoyed controlling her men. A little bit of lacerating pleasure—and then she'd slow things down—until Fargo's entire body was pleading with her for satisfaction.

She spent a little more time on driving him crazy by manipulating him in various ways—she was particularly adept at wrapping her hair around him and rubbing it across the tip of his sex—and then mounting him without letting him in very far.

She rolled off him and grabbed his wand and spread her legs wide so that she could wrap herself around him when he got inside her. "I prefer the missionary position," she joked. "It must be my upbringing as a minister's daughter."

They then proceeded to do some holy rolling. He put it to her on the hay, on the rough timber of the loft, against the wall, and then back to the hay again. He couldn't ever remember being with a woman who could keep up with him. Every few minutes she reached a new climax. She hadn't been kidding. She had plenty more where that came from.

They ended up with her arms stretched out against the wall and him taking her from the back, their scents and sounds so intermingled they seemed as one now, her doing a dance on his shaft with her hips that the native girls you read about in books could only dream about.

He literally drove her up the wall as he penetrated ever deeper, so that she grabbed for cuts and nicks in the wood to lift herself up the slanting barn.

At the very last moment, knowing he was about to explode she had a surprise for him. She wriggled away from him and then turned on him and took his massive joint in her hands, guiding the whole of it into her mouth. The feeling was a light show of colors and images and sensations that seemed to touch every single pore on his body. She kept licking and licking him long after he'd spent himself . . .

What neither of them knew was that they had an audience. There in the far, shadowy corner on the floor below, crouched on ground that rats had pebbled with their feces—there crouched Michael. Hearing it all.

With everything Fargo had heard about him, he'd been expecting Reverend Amis to be this towering, messianic figure. He was instead a mild-looking, handsome man with graying dark hair and dressed in a flannel shirt, denim jacket, and denim pants. He looked like a cowboy. He carried a Sharps in one hand and the bloody remains of three rabbits in the other. He carried them by their feet, red streaks running down his arm and dripping to the ground below, as he stood silent and watched the two lovers as they descended the ladder. He cleared his throat, alerting them to his presence.

The girl jumped down and blurted, "I wasn't talking to him, honest I wasn't."

Amis shook his head. "Calm down, Grace. You'll give our guest the wrong impression here. He'll think I'm some kind of ogre." He kept his tone light, almost joking. He walked over to Fargo and held up the rabbits for inspection. "Like rabbit, do you, Mister Fargo?"

"I like mine cooked a little better than that," Fargo said, "and how do you know my name?"

"I know many things," Amis said. "God keeps me informed." Then, "Grace, you take these up and get them all trimmed out."

"Yessir." She seemed visibly relieved that Amis

hadn't blamed her for Fargo showing up here unannounced.

She took the rabbits from the reverend, smearing her hand with blood in the process. She brushed away some of the flies that had settled on the carcasses. Then she recklessly took a last look at Fargo.

As she walked away, Fargo did his best not to take notice of her backside, but that was impossible. She was just too fetching to look away from.

Amis went over to a well, pumped up some water, and washed blood and hair and flecks of rabbit meat off his hands. "So how may I help you, Mister Fargo? Have you come here to turn your life over to God?"

"Not quite yet. I'm wondering if any of your flock hates Noelle's customers enough to kill them?"

"You mean, do *I* hate Noelle enough to try and run her out of business?"

"If you want to start out with yourself, fine by me. Do you hate her that much?"

"I hate the sin, not the sinner. It's her sinning that gives me sleepless nights, not her, personally."

"Do you hate her sin enough to kill off some of her customers?"

Amis smiled. "Nothing subtle about you, is there, Fargo?"

"I'm not good at what you'd call the social graces. If I want to ask something, I ask it."

Amis wiped his hands on his trousers. "I understand that you're a friend of hers."

"Not really. I'm just helping her out."

"And now she's hiring you to protect her from the great unknown. That's what's really frightening, isn't it, Mister Fargo? It must drive her crazy. Walking around town day after day and realizing that anybody she passes in the street could be responsible for killing her customers and trying to drive her out of business."

"So neither you nor your flock have anything to do with trying to shut her down?"

"We picket and we pray. Have you ever been in a saloon on a Friday night and watched all the workingmen drink up their paychecks instead of take them home to their good wives? It's a sickening spectacle, Mr.

Fargo. And it's all the worse when you add gambling to it. Their checks go twice as fast. That's why the casinos try and stick together. They know that if we can drive one of them out then we can eventually drive all of them out. I should say 'knew.' Now we're down to one. Noelle's. You'll forgive the tone of satisfaction in my voice."

"The workingmen aren't responsible for themselves?" Fargo said. "My understanding is that the Lord gave us free will."

"Free will, yes," the reverend said, warming to the possibility of a theological discussion. "But that includes the will to tempt other men with whiskey and women and the prospect of easy money at the gaming tables. If you removed the temptation, the men would go home to their wives and children."

"Grace said you knew Suzanna. Know much about her?"

"Suzanna was a good girl. Hers was a hard road, but she was cleansed of her past before passing. In fact, we stood right here on the grass many nights, talking. She loved to look at the moon. She said she was raised in an orphanage and that one of her few pleasures was looking out the window at night after all the other kids had gone to sleep. She said they always picked on her. But when they were asleep she had the window and the moon all to herself and it was very peaceful. She said she hated it in town at the casino because she didn't have a window there and didn't have any way of seeing the moon for herself."

"She told you about her past?"

Reverend Amis studied Fargo a moment. "I'm not sure what you're looking for."

"A man named Philly is missing. I think he left because he knew something about her."

"Like what?"

"That," Fargo said, "is what I was hoping you'd tell me."

"Well, I can't go into any detail. She told me everything about herself, I believe. But I suppose I can tell you a few general things."

"Such as?"

"She came to town here looking for somebody."

"Did she find him?"

"That's about all I can say about that. I do know there was one man she was afraid of."

"Who?"

"Noelle's husband, Rick."

"What did he do to her?"

"Nothing specific. He was just always sniffing around her. Hinting that he knew her secret."

"What kind of secret?"

"That's all I can say. I've said too much already."

Fargo saw Grace peeking out from inside the cabin. She was hiding just inside the door. He kept thinking about what she'd said—that she knew things that could get the reverend in serious trouble.

He said, "Well, Reverend, if you hear anything—if the Lord happens to whisper something in your ear— I'd appreciate you sharing it with me."

"I wouldn't scoff about the Lord whispering secrets to His chosen ones. It happens all the time."

"Tell me, how does the Lord feel about men of the cloth who keep bleeding their flock for every last penny because they're too lazy to go out and work?"

The reverend flushed. Anger came quickly to his eyes. You could see him consciously restraining himself from giving a sharp answer. "Has anybody ever told you how insolent you are, Mister Fargo?"

"Not long ago, as a matter of fact." He glanced to the cabin again. Grace was just disappearing behind the door. He gave the minister a jaunty little salute and said, "You know, you didn't exactly deny that you're the one who's been killing Noelle's customers."

The reverend had regained his composure. He smiled slyly. "No, I guess I never did, did I?"

Fargo went over and mounted up. Grace snuck a last look at him and Fargo at her. She ducked back behind the doorway just as the reverend started to walk to the cabin.

Fargo was halfway back to town when somebody fired on him from behind. The shot hadn't been meant as a warning. The shot had been meant to kill.

Fargo tumbled from his horse and rolled across the mud into the tall grass. Two more rifle shots came in quick succession. He rolled himself farther back so that he was now in the timber.

He yanked his Colt free and began scanning the road behind him. The hill he'd just come down was the most likely vantage point for the shooter. Somewhere up there in that tangle of pine and long grasses.

The shooter was out of range for Fargo to fire back effectively. All he could do was stay crouched there and hope the shooter didn't get lucky.

But then Fargo heard a sound that was a whole lot scarier than a rifle firing at him. The low, throbbing sound—not a roar, but a deep, trembling purrlike sound that Fargo could literally feel in his bones—transformed the timberlands into a hunting preserve for the biggest cat in the West.

Somewhere above him, no doubt peering down from a heavy branch, was the puma whose tracks he'd seen on the road. Pumas didn't like humans who trespassed on ground the animals had marked as their own. It would help if they'd post No Trespassing signs, but it was a little late for that.

The shooter chose this moment to squeeze off a few more rounds. These came damned close to creasing Fargo's hat. He had to duck away from the bullets—but do so in a way that wouldn't give the puma a reason to charge.

A heavy animal scent filled the air now. Saliva, urine, body heat, and probably blood from its most recent kill were the elements of the stench.

Fargo turned slowly, carefully, to get a look at his new foe. He couldn't see the big cat, not at first. The animal was concealed in the heavy branches of the forest. Then, through a small open patch between several hardwoods, he saw the face of the puma. Its lips were drawn back from razorlike teeth as the purring sound pulsated throughout the forest.

From what Fargo could see, the cougar was tawny in color and maybe five feet long. The odd sweetness of the face told him that this was a female. She might well have cubs nearby and be protecting them.

81

She played a psychological game with Fargo. She let out a shriek that raised goosebumps on his arms and the back of his neck. Cougars were famous for this. There'd been warriors in the misty eons of early history who'd used sound to do the same thing. The Celts had scared off many adversaries simply by standing on the outskirts of an encampment and making cries that frightened even the boldest of warriors. "Were-music" it had been called by the Normans, who admitted that they frequently ran away without fighting when they heard such cries. All this contributed to the useful myth—useful to the Celts—that these warriors were not quite of human origin.

The cry of the cougar, or the mountain lion as it was known in some circles, was sometimes a warning for the opponent to flee—or a signal that the cougar was about to attack.

The animal would have no trouble diving through the branches and swooping down on Fargo. And Fargo knew it.

While there was no natural sound Fargo could make that would drive the animal away, there was another sound available that would make the cougar understand that Fargo was just as deadly as the beast.

The cougar's cry again.

The limb it rested on shook slightly as it took a few steps forward. Fargo imagined the animal landing on him with all its ferocity and power, using its huge claws both like clubs and knives. The cougar would throw Fargo to the ground and literally rip him apart.

There was one chance to avoid this confrontation. Fargo hoped it would work. He didn't blame the beast for distrusting the two-legged one whose weapons brought thunder and death. The puma, according to many of the tribes Fargo had learned from, had as much right to the land as mankind did. Fargo saw no reason to argue with this belief.

The branch wiggled again, leaves rattling.

Fargo knew this would be his last chance. If he didn't act now, he would be battling the cougar within moments.

He fired three quick shots at an angle into the air.

There was a long, silent moment, followed by great agitation in the tree that partially hid the cougar.

Then the cougar moved. Fargo could imagine the image in the beast's mind—the image of the two-legged ones who had slain so many of the other cougars. The animal bound from one tree to the next. And then from that tree to the next. And so on until the great Oregon forest was silent again.

It was a good thing he'd thought to use his gun to scare the cougar away, Fargo thought. Otherwise, the animal would have been down on him for sure.

He was careful leaving the timberland. The shooter might still be nearby, lurking, waiting for his chance. But this time there was no gunfire. Fargo mounted his horse and rode off.

An hour later, Fargo walked into his hotel, nodded to the clerk and angled his steps to the right.

"Maybe you forgot, Mister Fargo," said the clerk helpfully. "You're on the second floor."

"I need to see the owner."

He knew the clerk would protest so he walked faster. "But Mr. Tolliver is—"

Fargo hurried down the hall and knocked on the owner's door.

"Yes."

"It's Skye Fargo."

"Oh, yes, just a minute, Mister Fargo."

This time, the man was dressed in a white collarless shirt, a vest, and dark trousers. "I hope you find the accommodations satisfactory."

The accommodations are fine, Fargo thought, thinking of sweet little Doris. "I wanted to talk to you about one of your guests."

"Why, of course, come in and have some coffee with me."

The man got around his room with amazing speed and agility. He didn't bump into, or even nudge anything as he went to a table, poured Fargo a cup of coffee, and then brought it back. Tolliver had a cup of his own coffee waiting for him on the arm of a chair. He sat down with a sigh and said, "So how can I help you?"

"I'm betting you keep up on things around here."

Tolliver smiled. "People tell blind people all sorts of things. I guess they think we're 'safe' somehow. The truth is, blind people are some of the biggest gossips I know." He laughed. "Me included."

Fargo laughed with him. "I'll remember that the next time I'm tempted to tell a blind person all my secrets." He sipped the steaming coffee. "This is very good."

"My late wife's special recipe, God love her. She was blind, too. I became a gossip and she became a cook. Now, what can I do for you, Mister Fargo?"

"You had a guest here, Suzanna—"

Tolliver stopped him even before he could get the last name out. "She radiated beauty. I'm a lonely, old man, but she made me feel young again. She'd come down here sometimes and talk to me. I don't know why she worked at that casino. She was way too refined for that. But she had a mission of some kind—"

"A mission?"

"Something she'd come here to Cumberland to find out."

"Something—or somebody?"

"That's a good way to put it, Mister Fargo. She tried to convince me that she'd come here strictly by chance. Just looking around for someplace to settle. And just happened to stumble on Cumberland. But I never believed that for a second. Not a second."

"Did you get any sense of why she came out here?"

"No specific sense. But it was something that made her very angry. She was so warm and lovely most of the time—but every once in a while, I'd hear this rage—I know she spent a lot of time with Philly and Bowen. I think she even made a few trips with them to that 'bo jungle out under the trestle bridge. I'm sure they'd tell you the same thing. Then all of a sudden—no matter what you were talking about—she'd get very angry. A cold anger. The kind that's been with you a long, long time. The kind you can control until you find the person you want to let it loose on. And then God help that person."

"She have any other friends in town? I know Doris here liked her very much."

Tolliver chuckled. "And Doris tells me that she likes you very much, Mr. Fargo."

"You don't miss anything, do you?"

"Not a trick," the blind man said proudly. "Not a single trick." Then: "You know, who she got to be friends with was Fiona."

"Fiona? That surprises me."

"It shouldn't. Not when you think about it. Fiona is a refined woman—and so was Suzanna."

"I'll have to ask Fiona about her."

Tolliver sipped more coffee. "You've made me curious, Mister Fargo. I'm assuming you're trying to find out who killed McCarey and almost killed you. But what does any of that have to do with Suzanna?"

"I'm not sure . . . yet."

"Do you believe she committed suicide?"

"No."

"Good," said Tolliver. "Because neither do I." He nodded with great pleasure. "Keep up your investigation, Mister Fargo. I think you're getting somewhere."

10

Fargo's next stop was Fiona's house.

The Mexican lady answered the door. She did not seem unduly happy to see Fargo. She said she would see if "the lady" would agree to see him. She didn't invite him in. He stood on the porch, enjoying the thin but pleasant sunshine. A squirrel watched him. He watched the squirrel right back.

The Mexican woman opened the door, moving her bulk so that he could step inside. She didn't say a word, simply led him through the ornately decorated house—princes probably lived in such a place—with its winding staircase, flocked wallpaper, and myriad wall fixtures, and into a sunny square room that served as a study.

Fiona Caine sat in her wooden wheelchair in a prim blue dress with a high collar. Her lovely hair was pulled back into a chignon. She was elegant, sophisticated, and could easily have passed for her sister, Noelle.

"Friendly lady," Fargo said, as the maid left.

Fiona laughed. She had a good one. "She intimidates me, too, and I'm supposed to be her boss. Would you like some coffee?"

"That sounds good. I can get it."

"Don't make me feel helpless, Skye. I can get it."

And so she did, moving easily across the parquet floor to a small table where a china coffeepot sat next to matching cups and saucers. She poured him a cup and wheeled it back to him. The room suited her. Formal, dignified, filled with leather bound books and classical statuary. She seemed at home here. Hard to imagine she'd ever worked in a casino. Even though she was Noelle's twin, Skye sensed that she was very different from her sister.

"I don't like to feel helpless, Skye."

"I don't blame you."

"This is quite a house."

"Noelle furnished it for me."

"Think she'd do one for me?"

"The way she was talking about you last night," Fiona said, "I think she'd be happy to *build* you a house. She's very taken with you, you know."

"And I'm very taken with both of you."

He realized he'd said the wrong thing when Fiona's mouth tightened. He remembered the rumors that she'd been sleeping with Noelle's husband.

He said, "Bradshaw wants me to leave town."

"You don't seem like the kind of man who'd let Bradshaw push you around."

"I'm not."

"Good."

"But I need your help."

She seemed to sense right away that his request would make her uncomfortable. "I'm not going to like this, am I?"

"Probably not. But I need to know some things."

She nodded, then sipped her own coffee and stared out the window a moment. "I dream about running. You take things for granted all your life. That you can run. And when you can't—" She turned back to him. "You want to know who shot me."

"Or who you think might have shot you."

"All right. First of all, I don't think it was Noelle."

"Why not? If you were sleeping with Rick, she'd have a good reason."

"I was sleeping with Rick and she did have a good reason, but she didn't shoot me. She had every reason to hate me, but she also loved me. And still does. As I love her. We're sisters and that's a very strong bond to break."

"Did Rick shoot you?"

"Why would Rick shoot me?"

"Maybe he felt spurned. Maybe he felt that since

she'd found out about you two, you wouldn't want him anymore."

"I didn't want him any more, as a matter of fact. My fiance had died of smallpox and I was so distraught I couldn't even get out of bed most days. Rick started coming around to see me. I knew he was trying to seduce me—that's how the Ricks of the world spend their lives, testing out female conquests—but I didn't care. I was just glad for the company. Rick is very clever. And amusing. But I let things go too far. It was all my fault. I could've stopped it before it got out of hand but I didn't. Maybe secretly I wanted Noelle to feel as bad as I did. I don't know why I slept with him. And I probably never will. All I know is that I practically destroyed my sister. I hope someday she'll be able to forgive me, even though I don't deserve it."

No tears. Not even a frown. But her remorse was in her voice. A remorse that was always there, he realized now. Sometimes in life you do something that you regret so much—that shames you so much—that you can never quite let go of it, that always stays there with you.

She smiled sadly. "As for Rick, by then he'd gone on to Suzanna Tolan. Or tried to. I don't think he got very far."

That name again, Fargo thought. "I keep hearing about her. Sounds like she must've been very beautiful."

"Very beautiful—and very mysterious. She was far too refined to work in a casino and yet that's just what she did. Several very prominent bachelors wanted to marry her, even after she'd been working for us. By then I suppose she was something of a soiled dove. But they didn't care. Bradshaw despised her. He tried to run her out of town several times."

"For what reason?"

She shook her head. "Who knows. By then Reverend Tyler had his ear. Tyler thought she was a bad example for young women. A girl of obvious breeding—and yet she chose to work with us. So Bradshaw got on his high horse, too."

"Everybody says it was suicide."

"I'm sure it was. She was a very high-strung young

woman. She had terrible black moods she couldn't control. I felt sorry for her."

He said, "Then do you have any idea who shot you?"

"An idea. No evidence."

"Who?"

"Reverend Tyler."

"Why would he shoot you?"

"Drive us away. He couldn't seem to get rid of us any other way. Or the other two casinos, either. I think he thought that he could scare us away. I don't think he meant to just cripple me, either. I think he meant to kill me. But I didn't die."

"I met him. He was a lot more mild-mannered than I would have thought."

She smiled. "Just be careful of his son. He's the one that gets that whole congregation stirred up. Just watch yourself. I'm sure Tyler's behind the three murders, too. Tyler or his people. When I say Tyler I actually mean anybody associated with his church. They're fanatics. And very scary. The things they do to their poor little children to keep them in line—" She shook her elegant head. "Just be careful, Skye."

He set down his coffee cup. Got up. Walked over to her. Shook her slender hand. "I appreciate your honesty, Fiona."

"Thanks. It actually helps me to talk about it sometimes. Like the way Catholics go to confession, I guess." Then she smiled. "Just watch out for Michael. People say he's demonic."

Fargo wondered what was going on. A mortuary wagon was parked at an angle in front of his hotel. A small clutch of people watched him with great curiosity as he crossed the street to the boardwalk in front of the place.

"You heard the news yet, Fargo?" one of the onlookers asked.

"No."

The onlooker grinned. "Don't worry. You will."

The desk clerk was talking to the deputy Fargo had fought with. The deputy glowered at him. So did the desk clerk.

"What's going on here?" Fargo asked.

"Go ask the sheriff," the deputy said.

Fargo went up the steps, now getting a bad feeling in his stomach. Things just kept on getting worse in this place.

It appeared that most of the people in the hotel, including the help, were crowded into the narrow second-floor hallway outside Fargo's room. Bradshaw stuck his whiskey-blotched face out of Fargo's door and said, "Well, well. Look who we have here. Get your ass inside, Fargo."

"So you knew Philly."

"Yes, I knew him."

"And you killed him."

"Very clever, Bradshaw. But unfortunately for you, the answer is no, I didn't kill him."

"When was the last time you saw him?"

"When I was trying to help him out the other night."

"Why were you trying to help him out?"

"I'd made some money outriding. I make a point of trying to help people out whenever I have a little extra."

"You're going to make me cry, Fargo."

Fargo sat in a chair with his feet up on the bureau. He had the door closed. He'd answered a few questions at first, but the crowd in the hall got him down. There was too much eagerness in their voices. They didn't give a damn about Philly. They just wanted the sordid details. Apparently, though they lived in a town where violent death was not exactly uncommon, they just couldn't get enough of it. You could keep your dance hall girls, give them a corpse any day. Some town.

Fargo was more interested in the two muddy boot tracks that didn't seem to interest Bradshaw at all. Spanish-cut boots. You saw a lot of them in California, because of all the Spanish culture there. But not so many in Oregon Territory.

"How'd Philly get in your room here, Fargo?"

"I have no idea."

"Why'd he come to see you?"

"I have no idea."

"So Philly comes up here and lets himself in—since

90

you say you weren't here to let him in—and somebody kills him."

"That's how I'd read it."

"Well, that isn't how I read it at all, Fargo."

Fargo wondered again how, in fact, Philly had come to be in his room. And why. Had Philly decided that whatever he knew was just too dangerous and that he had to share it with somebody?

Fargo needed to look up Bowen and see if he knew what was going on.

"You must like dead people, Fargo," Bradshaw said. "You sure seem to spend a lot of time with them."

"Before you ask me again, I didn't kill him. And I don't know who did. And I don't know how he got into my room or why." Fargo turned around in his chair and looked at the towering lawman. "That should pretty much wrap it up."

"This won't be wrapped up until you're hanging from a nice, sturdy oak branch."

Bradshaw went about his work. He examined Philly from several angles. Somebody had shot him in the forehead. Bradshaw walked over to the window, leaned against the glass, and gaped up and down the fire escape. He tried the lock on the window. It had been painted shut. "He didn't get in that way."

"He got into my room," Fargo said, "without knowing somebody was following him."

"And this somebody—he or she was the killer?"

"Of course," Fargo said. "By the way, anybody hear any gunshots?"

"The men on either side of this room claim they were gone."

"What's 'claim' supposed to mean?"

"It means they don't want to get involved in a murder case."

Bradshaw inspected the closet. He went through the bureau, drawer by drawer. He got down on his knees—the bones of which made cracking sounds almost as sharp as gunshots—and inspected the floor. When he was on his feet again, he said, "Why'd you kill him, Fargo?"

"You know better than that, Bradshaw."

"No, I don't."

A knock. Bradshaw went to the door. The deputy Fargo had battled with came in. He scowled when he saw Fargo. The man's nose was swollen and he had a black eye. He was a tall, wide, bull-strong man with the face of every bully in the land. Bullies were not known for losing graciously.

"I don't think you two have ever been properly introduced," Bradshaw said, amused by the two men facing each other.

"You've got one hell of a good puncher there," Fargo said to Bradshaw.

"You got lucky is all," the deputy said to Fargo.

"Ken Stalling, I believe you've met Mister Fargo here." Bradshaw still sounded sardonic.

"Yeah, I have. And I'll meet him again sometime. You can count on it."

"Sounds like I'm going to need legal protection, Sheriff," Fargo said.

"Well, you're not going to get it from me," Bradshaw said. "I told you I wanted you out of this town. But it looks like you stayed long enough to hang yourself."

"That's what I wanted to know, Sheriff," Stalling said. "Should I go get the doctor?"

"Yeah. He'll need to make a report."

"What about him?" Stalling said. "Should I handcuff him?"

There was a knock. But the caller did not wait for a response, merely pushed open the door and stepped in. For the second time—and in the nick of time—Prescott G. Withers stepped into Fargo's life.

"Good timing, Withers," Fargo said. "They were just about to lynch me."

"Don't give me any ideas, Fargo," Bradshaw said.

"They seem to think that just because there's a corpse in my room, I had something to do with it."

"There you go again," Withers said to Bradshaw, picking up on Fargo's ironic tone, "jumping to conclusions."

"You two go right ahead and have your fun," Bradshaw said. "I'll have the last laugh when they're putting the noose around his neck."

Fargo said, "I didn't kill him."

Stallings said, "You were looking all over town for him. And I got a dozen witnesses who'll say so."

"I'd like to see the law that equates looking for somebody with killing him," Withers said.

"He was in the room," Bradshaw said. "Fargo's room."

"He was obviously shot," Withers said. "Was he shot with Fargo's gun?"

He was a wily old codger, Fargo thought. Not even Fargo himself had thought of that. He got up and walked over to where Philly lay. The body had begun to smell. At least, he'd died with some decent clothes on. And shaved. And all scented up with bay rum. He'd spent his last hours as a respectable man.

Withers produced a pencil. He used it as a pointer. He walked over to the body and pointed to the bullet hole in the forehead. "You know a lot about guns, Sheriff Bradshaw."

"A fair amount."

"What sort of gun do you own, Fargo?" Withers said. Fargo showed him.

"A Colt," Withers said. "Now, as you'll notice, Sheriff, the hole this bullet left in the forehead is very small."

Once again, Fargo watched the demonstration of Withers's consummate courtroom skills.

"He could've used a different gun," Bradshaw said.

"True," Withers said. "But then it would be encumbent upon you—as the representative of the law in this town—to find that different gun, wouldn't it?"

"You sonofabitch," Bradshaw said.

"You're always talking about law and order, Sheriff," Withers said. "You have order. The town is peaceful at the moment. What I want is law—justice—for my client. Until you can find the murder weapon and prove that he used it, you can't in good conscience—or in law—charge him with the murder of this man." Withers did a double-take. "My God, I hadn't even noticed. It's Philly. In all the years I've seen him around, I've never seen him cleaned up this way."

"That's another thing," Bradshaw said. "Where did he get the money to get all spiffed up this way?"

Withers smiled. "I'm sure, in the course of your professional and thorough investigation, you'll find the answers to all these questions. Now, if you don't mind, my client and I would like to go to the café and have some coffee. C'mon, Fargo, we've taken up enough of their valuable time. They have work to do."

Fargo was stunned by the brazen attitude the lawyer had struck. Moments later, they were headed out the door and making their way through the tight knot of people filling the hall.

Bradshaw was no doubt back in the murder room with his jaw agape, trying to figure out what the hell that damned old lawyer had just done to him.

"Did you really want to get some coffee?" Fargo said when they reached the street.

"No," said Withers. "I just wanted to get you out of that room before Bradshaw got any fancy notions about arresting you."

Fargo smiled. "That's what I figured. I appreciate it. I want to go look up Philly's friend Bowen."

"Be careful, Fargo," Withers said. "The man is a liar through and through. I had to represent him in a case once—nobody else would—he got himself accused of breaking into a place. I got him off. But I knew all the time he was guilty. That man never speaks a word of truth."

Fargo thanked the man again and then headed down near the railroad spur to where the hobos lived beneath the bridge. On a chilly but sunny autumn day like this one, even the tin and tarpaper shacks didn't look so bad. Some of the 'bos had made a huge pot of stew. It smelled good. A clothesline was covered with shirts and jackets and trousers that had been washed in the creek. A couple of 'bos were scraping long-handled razors over their faces. The razors were the weapon of choice in hobo jungles.

The encampment consisted of eight small shacks and several tents. There was a freshly dug latrine to the west and a windbreak of pine and cedar to the east. Far up on a hill, outlined against the sun, stood a sentry with a rifle. Bradshaw's men, railroad dicks and local citizens groups opposed to hobos on general principles no doubt paid the encampment visits from time to time. The men had learned the hard way to have an early warning system.

Fargo went to the tin shack where Bowen slept. He threw back the blanket that served as a door and peered inside. The odors nearly knocked him down. Sleep, sweat, bad liquor, tobacco. The place was empty. He started to go inside and look around, but heard something behind him.

When Fargo pulled his head from the shack and turned around, a hairy, shirtless man about the size of a boxcar stood a few feet away. He held a long wooden club in one hand and kept slapping it against the open palm of his other hand. "You law?"

"Not hardly."

"What you want here?" The way he spoke, Fargo knew that he was what people called "slow." That didn't make him any less dangerous. The man's face and chest was a crosshatch of scars. This was a man who'd tasted the straight razor many times. Fargo imagined he had shared that taste with many others, too.

"I'm looking for Bowen."

"He ain't here."

"Yeah. I can see that."

"I don't like you."

Fargo almost laughed. The bruiser's voice had a surly quality that was comic.

"Well, gosh," Fargo said, "I'm awful sorry to hear that."

"Kincade!" a colored man shouted. He was coming fast from the direction of the creek. "Kincade! He's Philly's friend! He's all right—don't hurt him!"

The man was skinny and quick. His dark eyes shone with all the intelligence poor Kincade lacked. "Sorry, mister."

"It's all right," Fargo said. "No harm done."

The man slid his arm through Kincade's and angled him gently away from Fargo, leading him to the large pot of stew boiling above the fire. "There's bread and stew for you, Kincade. You just settle down now, all right? You don't want to get all worked up, remember?" He spoke as he would to a small child.

The man got Kincade fixed up with a bowl of stew and some bread and then came back to Fargo. "I'm Robbins." They shook hands.

"Thanks for helping me out."

"He pitched off a train the wrong way when he was about sixteen. Landed on his head. Sounds funny to say, Mister Fargo. But that's jest what happened. He ain't been right since. You gotta be careful around him because he can go mean on you all of a sudden. And when Kincade goes mean on you, Lord help you. I'm about the only one who can calm him down, it seems. I'm sorta his keeper. I don't mind, I guess, except when he starts callin' me 'coon' and names like that. Then I mind."

"Too bad he can't appreciate what you do for him," Fargo said, "I'm looking for Bowen."

"He didn't come back last night."

"He ever miss nights like that?"

Robbins shook his head. "Not that I know of."

"He have any place to stay in town?"

"Nope. He don't have any more money than the rest of us."

"I don't suppose you'd let me look through his shack."

Robbins frowned. "Now you can answer your own question on that one, can't you, Mister Fargo?"

Fargo smiled. "Yeah, I probably can."

" 'Bout the only things 'bos have is their honor. You start rattin' each other out—or helpin' the enemy—and you got yourself a big pot of trouble, Mister Fargo."

"It was worth a try." He followed Robbins's gaze. Kincade was eating his stew and talking to the other two 'bos standing over him. They were glaring in Fargo's direction.

"You'd best be going, Mister Fargo. People here ain't real keen on visitors. 'Specially them two with Kincade over there. They just love to fight. And they're good at it. And if one can't do it alone, they don't have no problem doublin' up on a man."

A gambler like the Trailsman always played the odds.

There was no way he was going to get into Bowen's shack. So what was the point of fighting it out with two men who'd pull razors on him?

He thanked Robbins and left.

Three hours into looking for Bowen, Fargo heard a name that was new to him. New and interesting. Ruth Ellen Patterson. The name had been given him by a sot who said he'd known Philly well and that Philly always talked about liking "the hefty ones" and that Ruth Ellen was just about as hefty a gal as a man could possibly want. Fargo got his Ovaro from the livery and rode on out to what should have been called kitty-city.

Fargo couldn't ever recall seeing this many felines. The house wasn't all that much bigger than a shed nor a whole hell of a lot nicer than one of the shacks in 'bo town. But the cats . . .

They were of every size, color, and breed. The tykes tumbled in play while the older ones sat on tree stumps, porch steps, open areas in the grass, and even up in the trees looking at everything with majestic indifference. I don't know about your shit, Fargo, but mine don't stink. That was what he read in their green enigmatic gazes.

He knocked several times, but there was no answer. He didn't want to have to come back here so he took the chance of opening the door and going inside.

Fargo reckoned he'd never seen a woman of this size naked before. And he wasn't real sure he ever wanted to again, either.

But first things first. He could be critical of her size later.

The "house" was a one-room cabinlike affair. The furniture—especially the horsehair couch—was of a quality he wouldn't have expected. But right now even the most expensive furniture wouldn't have looked so good. Somebody had ransacked the place, looking for something. Littered the floor, thrown all sorts of things into piles.

The woman groaned.

Fargo went over to the basin and dipped a rag into the tepid water. He brought it back and began daubing her face with it.

Her unexpected shriek sent him a good foot into the air. He'd never heard a human soul shriek like that. A shriek like that would scare the hell out of any ghosts and goblins you cared to name.

Her deep-blue eyes came open and she said, "I'm naked!"

"I know you're naked."

"I'm so ashamed of my fat body that I—" She touched a hand to her head. "Oh, my God, this is so humiliating. There's a robe over there in the corner—"

He found it, gave it to her, helped her on her feet, into the black cotton robe.

"Don't look at me," she said.

"Look," he said, "there's blood on the side of your head. You're hurt."

"I'm hurt, all right. Hurt right here." She touched her heart. "You're going to tell everybody what I look like naked, aren't you?"

"Not if you don't want me to. By the way, are you Ruth Ellen Patterson?"

"Who the hell else would I be?"

Easy to get along with, she wasn't.

"My name's Fargo."

"I'm not open to business to you, Fargo. Not ever. I don't let nobody see me naked, ever."

He said carefully, "But they told me in town you're—"

"They told you in town I was a crib girl. And that's true. But I'll let you know one thing. Nobody ever sees me naked."

"What about your customers?"

"I only work at night. And with the lantern off." She hesitated. Tears coursed down her cheeks. "And now you've seen me—"

He felt sorry for her. She really was embarrassed and ashamed. The thing was, Fargo had much more to worry about than her vanity. He said, "Who knocked you out?"

"He had a mask on. I don't know." She was still crying, though forcing herself to stop.

"What did he want?"

"He thought Philly left something here the night he stayed."

"Philly stayed here? When?"

"Last night. Why?"

She obviously hadn't heard about Philly. "He's dead. Murdered. Somebody killed him in my room."

"Murdered!" She gasped, then frowned. "How come you're involved in all this?" She kept cinching the belt on her robe tighter and tighter, as if the belt might help her shrink.

"That doesn't matter. Did the man say what he was looking for?"

"Just something that he thought Philly left here."

Fargo rubbed his jaw. "He was probably the killer. He must not have found what he was looking for on Philly's body."

"Well, Philly didn't leave nothing here."

"Did he tell you he'd come into money?"

"He didn't need to tell me. I could see for myself how cleaned up he was. New clothes and all. He was somethin' to see, he was."

"Tell me about what happened when he was here."

"Hey," she said. "I don't kiss and tell. I treat my men with respect."

"I don't mean the sex. I mean anything he might have said or did that might have given you an idea where his money came from all of a sudden."

"Oh," she said. She glanced around the mess her intruder had left her home in. Fargo was afraid she was going to start crying again. "Well, he didn't say nothing really." She paused. "Oh—wait. One thing was kinda interesting."

"What?"

"A couple of times—this was when he was gettin' pretty drunk—he said nobody'd believe who her father really was."

"Whose father who really was?"

She shrugged. "He never said." She looked at the debris covering her floor. "That bastard comes back here again, I'll make him get down on his hands and knees and lick that floor until it shines."

Fargo smiled.

"Don't laugh," she said. "I ain't just fat, Fargo. I got a lot of muscles, too. And if I ever see that sonofabitch again, I'm gonna use 'em on him. You wait and see."

Fargo decided now was a good time to leave before she made him get down on his hands and knees and do all sorts of things both natural and unnatural.

Fargo awoke to dusk, the last light of dying day faint in the window of his hotel room, moonlight already reflecting off the snow-covered mountain peaks.

He dressed and walked to the café where, as he ate his meal, he kept thinking about what Ruth Ellen had quoted Philly as saying—that nobody would believe who her father was. But who had he been talking about? And did it have any bearing on Philly's blackmail scheme?

He decided that Fiona might be able to help him. She'd known Philly. Maybe he'd said something to her, too. After his meal, he walked over to the Victorian house that looked gothic silhouetted against the full moon, spires and turrets recalling the splendid intrigue of foggy London town.

No lights shone downstairs, but for just a fleeting moment he thought he caught the shadow of a person in the narrow space between two drawn curtains. Probably the maid, kicking a puppy to death to get her nightly jollies.

Then the light went off on the second floor and almost at once the singing began. This was not a saloon song, either, but a popular ballad called "Moon of Hope" that had been part of a fashionable and long-running show Back East. Fargo didn't know anything about music, but he did know that singing this type of song took real talent. He wondered why all the lights had been snuffed out before the singing began. He also wondered who was singing. Whomever it was, she had a glorious voice and knew how to use it.

His first inclination was to knock on the front door, take his chances with the surly maid. But then he felt awkward about interrupting the singing. It grew more passionate by the moment. The woman was giving her voice a real workout with this piece of music.

He decided to walk around the house, see if he could

locate the area on the second floor where the music was coming from. Frost had already begun to shimmer on the autumn-brown grass. A dog sniffed around the grounds, looking lonely and cold.

The singing grew louder on the far side of the house—louder and more poignant. The song was about a woman who'd lost her lover. On nights of the full moon she imagined she saw his ghost standing on the ground outside her bedroom window. Fargo couldn't help but be drawn in by the power of the lyric and the sweet sense of loss in the singer's voice.

There was a fire escape built against the rear wall of the house. Probably had to be what with Fiona in a wheelchair. She would need a quick exit if fire ever struck.

Fargo glanced around quickly to see if anyone was looking. The house was isolated, no close neighbors. Plus a stand of pines stretching the width of the back lot gave him protection from curious eyes.

What if he climbed the fire escape to see what was going on? A thought kept coming back to him, one he'd rejected at first but now saw as a legitimate question that needed answering.

He began his ascent up the fire escape. The singing was loud enough that he didn't have to worry about being heard. The sniffing dog stood at the base of the fire escape, watching Fargo with great doggy curiosity. These human beings were interesting folk; no doubt about it.

The fire escape ended at a doorway. Made sense. In case of a fire, Fiona would be able to wheel herself to the door and slowly work her way down to the ground using her bottom and her arms. The chair would stay up here. It offered her at least the possibility of saving herself.

The door was unlocked. He eased his way in.

The scent of Fiona's intoxicating incense filled his nostrils. So did her perfume. The aromas created a perfect picture of her in his mind.

By now, he knew what he'd find. He tried two doors; one led to a large and fancy bedroom, and the other to a small room with a loom in it.

The third door was the one he wanted. The room was empty except for her wooden wheelchair. Ghostly white curtains fluttered on the breeze.

She was not only singing, she was dancing a kind of ballet that only emphasized the slender and elegant lines of her white naked body, which the moonlight stroked in silver splendor. Her red hair was a flame not only on her head but in the trim thatch at the top of her legs.

She wasn't aware of him for several minutes. He stood in the door watching her, his entire body stirring at the sight of such a lovely woman. His crotch was tight with need and desire and he found a fine sweat breaking on his face despite the slight chill in the house.

She was turning in her dance toward the window—still seemingly unaware of him—when finally she said, "Are you going to tell people my secret, Mister Fargo?"

Her question startled him. And then he laughed. "I could be bribed, I suppose."

She continued her pirouette. "And what would I bribe you with, Mister Fargo? Gold? Silver? Diamonds?"

"At the moment, I was thinking of something else."

"At the moment," she said, facing him boldly in her nakedness, "so was I."

And then, without him quite realizing it, she had crossed the floor and was in his arms.

She caressed his neck and shoulders as she kissed him, her fingers alive, cunning, magical. Then her right hand slipped downward and the tips of her fingers traced the length of his surging manhood. He bucked in response, his erection even bigger and harder now that she teased it with those fingers of hers.

She expertly slipped his rod free and began to play with it, meanwhile continuing to kiss him with a tongue as expert as her fingers. She took his thickened shaft and slid it between her legs, right against the warm, wet treasure between her legs. She was a brilliant tease, riding the length of him without quite letting him inside.

By now, Fargo was doing some teasing of his own, lashing her breasts and nipples with his tongue, never lingering on any one spot, writhing and gasping each time his tongue flicked on fresh skin.

She also had a sense of humor. She broke from him

and pulled him out of the room and down the hall, holding on to his throbbing sex as if it was a wagon handle.

Then they were naked in a canopied bed and there was nothing but deep shadow and the scent and thrill of her body. The tease continued as she forced him gently onto his back and began to use her tongue as he had used his—flicking, darting, lacing—but she went all up and down his body, while never once letting go of his swelling pole. He was damned near blind with the desire to shove himself inside her and feel the juicy heat of her sex.

Suddenly, she rolled off him and rolled on her side, lifting a leg so that he could kneel next to her and guide his steed inside. Which is just what he did. She was so silky wet she could take every greedy inch of him, crying out over and over as his rod drove deeper and deeper.

And then the dance began, him setting the pace with the rhythm of his thrusting and counterthrusting, his big left hand filling itself with her full breast, the nipple of which was as taut as a leather nub. Then it was his turn to roll her over and take her from the backside, her love canal steamy as a prehistoric jungle as he eased himself past the tangled web of her pubic hair and thrust himself inside for yet another ride.

He held her narrow hips and she went crazy on him, trying to fling herself every which way in response to the increasing pace of his thrusts. His grip on sanity wasn't all that strong, either, as he neared the threshold. He wanted to drive them both to an explosive numbing pleasure that would linger all night long.

This time, she leaned back, pushing him on to the bed so she could mount him. Her long hair whipped and lashed the winner home in this particular race. He leaned up to meet her breasts, teasing them again with his tongue, only making her inner thighs all the warmer and juicier with her pleasure. She reached the finish line throwing herself around with such violence he wondered for a moment if she were going to suddenly hurl herself out of bed. She clawed his chest, she bit his chin, she even nuzzled her face into the considerable hair under his arms, inhaling the manly perfume.

If they didn't reach their destination at the exact same moment, it was damned close. They were both caught up in the frenzy of their lust, him continuing to ram and jam himself up deeper and deeper inside her, her continuing to hold his hair so hard she was pulling out small tufts of it as her satisfaction reached a psychotic state.

And then they lay spent and sweaty and gasping . . .

"You want to tell me about it?" he said after a long while.

"About what?"

"Coy isn't my favorite style. You know damned well about what."

"I suppose you mean why am I faking my paralysis?"

"Good guess."

"Because she deserves it."

"She being—"

"Noelle, of course. She was cheating me at the casino. I couldn't prove it—I don't have half her brain when it comes to business. Noelle's as ruthless as I am, but she gets guilty about it. My fiancé was dead. I knew that if I faked my paralysis she'd take care of me the rest of my life. So I bribed the good doctor Givens to help me fake my paralysis. He shot me in the side so there'd be a wound in my back, but it'd heal right away without any permanent damage."

"Smart."

"And then I took up my role as the town cripple. A figure of piety and pity. People who used to despise me—and with good reason, I might add—couldn't stop themselves from fawning all over me like I was a pet animal or something. It got pretty funny sometimes. I could barely stop myself from laughing. And my dear sister was the worst of all. We'd always been competitive about everything. She even stopped cheating me of my half of the profits, the sweet thing. And now she's turned into a nun every time she's around me. She's devoted her entire life to me."

"That's pretty cruel."

"Maybe. She was cheating me, remember. But it's also boring. That's the worst part of all. Sitting in this damned chair all day. That's why I can't wait for night. Rosarita's gone and I can walk around the house. Even dance, the way I was tonight. Be like I used to be. Every so often, I have poor Noelle put me on a train. I always insist on going alone. I say I'm going to a clinic in Portland. But what I'm really doing is going there to raise hell for a week." She laughed again. "You wouldn't believe how much fun you can pack into seven days and seven nights."

"I believe it. Especially you."

"Yes, Skye, I have to admit. I am pretty good at being decadent when I want to be."

"I noticed."

She eased a silken hand over his manhood. Her fingers had magical powers. They revived his shaft instantly. If anything, it stood taller and prouder than it had during their first go-round.

She leaned over, brushing him with the fine fiery tangles of her red hair, and dragged a slow, sure tongue across the tip of his shaft. His whole body bucked in reaction.

"I see you're ready."

"You're damned right I am."

She lowered her head but this time he stopped her. "I need to ask you something."

"Can't it wait?" she said, gently stroking the formidable length of his shaft. "I think we have more important things to do first."

"I don't want anything but you on my mind while we're going at it again. So answer my question. Somebody told me that Philly said 'Everybody'd be real surprised if they knew who her father was.' Did he ever say anything like that to you?"

Her tongue lapped at him. "Oh, Skye, now's not the time to make me think about anything but you."

"I need to know. Just think a minute."

"Oh, you." She smiled up at him. "Can't you take pity on a poor crippled girl like me?"

"C'mon, now. Then we can have our fun."

She sat up, faking a pout. She was quite an accomplished faker. She sighed deeply, a child aggrieved by a parent making her do homework. "Tell me again what Philly said."

Fargo repeated it.

"That's odd."

"What is?"

"He actually did say something like that to me, come to think of it."

"When?"

She thought a moment. He was tempted to reach out and take one of her luscious breasts in his hand, but he knew this would only distract her. Still, that breast was damned tempting. An apple in Eden.

"The night before he died, I guess."

"Did he say anything else?"

"No. I asked him what he was talking about. But Philly was always very good at changing the subject when he wanted to."

"He'd never said anything like that to you before?"

"Not that I can recall."

"I wonder who he could've been talking about," Fargo said.

"With Philly, it's hard to tell. He knew everything and everybody. He covered the whole town. He could tell people things about their own family that shocked them. And sometimes he liked to do that. That was the only kind of power he had. Knowing things. And a lot of what he knew were things he shouldn't have known."

"Dangerous things?"

"Well," she said, "at least one of them was dangerous. It got him killed, didn't it?"

"Do you know his friend Bowen very well?"

She shook her head. "C'mon, Skye. You asked me your question about Philly. Now let's have some fun." To emphasize her point, she once again stirred him to stiff awareness with a single touch of her shamanic fingers.

"Just tell me about Bowen."

The prolonged and dramatic sigh. "I'm afraid of him. Philly was a pretty decent man—all things considered, I mean. But Bowen is a pure predator. I wouldn't be surprised if he killed Philly."

"You know, I was thinking the same thing myself."

"No more thinking, Skye. Now let's have some fun."

And before he could object in any way, she bent over and swallowed him right down to the hair on his crotch. She had set him on fire and he was loving it.

11

Down the street a dog was barking, hungry and lonely in the early morning fog, and Fargo knew what it felt like. So many things had been packed into the past twenty-four hours, he felt somewhat disoriented. He was certainly tired. It was funny in its way, though. He'd come to Cumberland to relax, and look at all that had happened to him.

The hotel lobby was empty except for the night clerk.

"Long night of it, huh, Mister Fargo?"

"Very."

"Hope you at least had some fun."

Fargo offered a weary smile. "Well, I sure tried, anyway."

Fargo walked to the stairs.

The night clerk said, "You had a visitor a while back."

"Oh? Who?"

"Man named Bowen. You know him?"

"He leave any message?"

"Just that he'd talk to you some time."

"That's all?"

"Afraid so, Mister Fargo."

Just then, the front door was thrown open with such force that it slammed against the wall. Two drunken drummers came in, arms around each other, each swinging a bottle of whiskey in the air. They were like skit comics—everything plaid; broad; and stereotypical, from their checkered suits to their derbies—and even their demand was familiar. "We, sir," said one of them to the night clerk, "demand a woman."

"Two women," the second drunk said, struggling to force two of his fingers up in the air. "Two. You got that?"

"I'm afraid that's not a service we provide our guests."

"He's snooty," the first drunk said.

"Very snooty," the second drunk said.

Fargo decided he'd had enough of this sparkling dialogue. He climbed the stairs to the second floor and walked quietly down the narrow hall to his room.

Bowen was waiting for him. He sat in a chair next to the window. He was angled in such a way that Fargo could see the knife that had been slammed deep into Bowen's chest. Fargo didn't even have to turn on the lamp to see the knife. It was there in silhouette against the lamplight of the street. Very dramatic. Maybe that's how the killer planned it. What good was murder if you couldn't be dramatic about it?

Fargo went over and went through Bowen's pockets. Bowen was starting to smell pretty sour. Bowen's pockets had been emptied. Fargo examined the hilt of the knife. Bone-handled. Nothing special or exceptional. Thousands like it on the frontier.

He closed his hotel door, locked it, and went downstairs. "There was an old black man here the other night. He sleep on the premises by any chance?"

"Yes, Mister Fargo, matter of fact, he does."

"You think he'd be mad if I woke him up and offered him five dollars to do a simple favor for me?"

"I sure wouldn't be mad if somebody woke me up and offered me five dollars. No, sir, I sure wouldn't."

"How do I get down there?"

The night clerk told him. Fargo followed his instructions, and by doing so came to a basement where three doors stood. He wanted the center one. He had to knock several times before he heard anybody stirring on the other side of the door.

The old man peered out and said, "Yes, sir?"

"I need somebody to run an errand for me. I'd pay you five dollars."

"Do you know what time it is, sir?"

"I believe it's around two in the morning."

"This wouldn't happen to be a dream, would it?"

Fargo laughed. "No, I'm afraid for both our sakes, it's not a dream."

"Then what would you like me to do for you, sir?"

"Do you know Prescott Withers?"

"If you mean the lawyer man, yessir, I know who he is."

"Do you know where he lives?"

"Yessir, it's a mighty fine house he has."

"I need you to go get him for me and bring him back here. Tell him Fargo said to come immediately."

The door hadn't opened beyond a slit all this time. There was just one brown eye watching Fargo all the time they talked.

"I won't get in no trouble?"

"No. None."

"And tell him to come back here?"

"That's right."

"And that Mr. Fargo needs to see him."

"Urgent," Fargo said.

"Urgent."

Fargo took some greenbacks from his pocket. It was twice as much as he'd promised. "How about I pay you even more. . . and I pay you right now?"

A black hand snaked through the slit in the door. "Yessir, I 'spect I could go wake up Mr. Withers. 'Lessen he tries to shoot me or somethin'."

"He won't. Now, can you leave right away?"

"Yessir. Right away."

Apparently, the old man considered their conversation over. He closed the door quietly. Fargo stood there a moment. He could hear the old man moving around on the other side of the door, scraping chairs, bumping into the wall. Getting ready.

One of the drummers who'd been wanting a woman was just walking through the back door, wiping his mouth with the back side of his hand. "Always feel better when I puke. Yes, indeed, I certainly do."

The man staggered through the front door. Fargo was glad he didn't have to spend a long time with these two. He went back up to his room. The door was still locked. He decided to leave it that way until Withers came.

He found a chair and sat down and took his Colt out and set it in his lap. This was some fine how-do-you-do. Not enough that somebody had planted one dead body in Fargo's room. Now the sonofabitch had planted another one. Withers would probably think this was some kind of a joke and that Fargo was involved in it somehow. Sheriff Bradshaw would be even worse about it. What the hell was going on here, anyway?

Fifteen minutes later he got the return on his ten dollar investment. "He says he's on his way," the old man huffed. "Didn't seem too happy about it."

"I don't blame him."

The man grinned. "Maybe I should've offered *him* five dollars."

Fargo could hear Withers's dramatic sounds downstairs. The man made slow progress up the steps. When he saw Fargo, he scowled. "Do you have any idea how old I am?"

"Pretty old."

"You think this is funny?" Withers hadn't dressed himself well. His vest was buttoned crooked and his Western hat was on backwards.

Fargo felt like a chastised schoolboy. "Nope. I rightly don't."

"I have rheumatism."

"I'm sorry."

"And arthritis."

"I'm sorry about that, too."

"And I don't sleep well as it is. And do you know why?"

"I guess not."

"Because, at my age, sleep reminds me of death. And so instead of sleeping, I lie there and wonder if I'll get buried alive. Or if there's an afterlife. Or if there's a hell, because if there is, that's surely where I am. Now aren't you sorry you had me woken up?"

Fargo laughed. "I sure as hell am."

Withers laughed, too. "Good. Now what can I do for you, Fargo?"

Fargo let him inside. Closed the door quietly. They spoke in whispers.

Fargo said, "Another one."

"My, my."

"Bradshaw's going to put me away for sure this time."

"He sure as hell is."

"But I have to tell him, don't I?"

Withers considered a moment. "You want me to say yes or no?"

"I'd rather have you say no."

"Then the answer's no."

"Good. Because I'm going to lock this door and get the hell out of here."

"And go where?"

"To talk to Rick Kingsley, for one thing."

"You think he killed Bowen here?"

"I think he's involved."

Fargo locked up and they walked downstairs.

"It's fun walking slow for an old man, eh, Fargo?" Withers said.

"I'll be an old man myself someday."

"No, you won't. Somebody'll shoot you before then."

"Is that a wish or a prediction?"

Withers grinned impishly. "Probably a little of both. Waking a poor old man like me up in the middle of the night."

"Poor old man, my ass," Fargo said. "You've got enough vinegar in you to poison anybody you bite."

Fargo saw that the old man got home safely. As they parted Fargo said, "Any idea where Rick Kingsley lives?"

"There's a place called the Rochester House for Gentlemen. Not that he's a gentleman of any description. He's got the upper west apartment. I happen to know that because my niece runs the place."

Ten minutes later, Fargo stood in an alley looking at the back of the new clapboard two-story house. White, it gleamed in the thin fog. There was both a front door and a back door. Fargo decided to take the latter. He had no trouble getting inside. The hall was dry and warm and smelled clean.

He worked his way up the stairs to the second floor, west end. He spent less than a minute letting himself in Kingsley's room. Snoring, damp and ridiculous, cut through the gloom. He started to close the door and then hesitated over something on the floor. Then he went in and stood in the darkness, letting his vision adjust to the shadows.

The apartment was two large rooms and looked to be nicely appointed. Rick Kingsley slept in a wide single bed. The furnishings looked to be standard but handsome.

There was a chair near Kingsley's bed. Fargo picked it up and brought it closer. He eased his Colt from its holster and pointed it directly at the sleeping man and said, "You sleep pretty well for a man with a guilty conscience."

Kingsley shot straight up in bed, a scream dying in his throat as he searched frantically around for the gun and holster that were supposed to be hanging from his bed post.

"I took the trouble of putting them on your bureau, Kingsley, so you wouldn't hurt yourself."

"You sonofabitch. First you screw my wife and now you steal my gun."

"At least I don't go around murdering people."

"Neither do I." Then, as if just realizing what Fargo had said, he said, "What the hell're talking about? I didn't murder anybody."

"So you say."

"Anyway, I could have you arrested for breaking in here."

"Then I'd have to tell Bradshaw about your blackmail scheme."

Kingsley reached over, took a half-smoked cigar from his night stand, struck a lucifer. The flame near his face revealed a man who'd had a lot to drink. "Murder, blackmail, breaking in here—you're crazy, Fargo. Now get the hell out of here."

"First you used Philly to do your dirty work. Then you used Bowen. That way, nobody would know it was you doing the blackmailing. You weren't in on the original scheme. Philly did that all by himself. He knew something about Suzanna. But he must've told you he was going to get rich or something. So you cut yourself in. Now, you're the only one left who knows the secret. That's a dangerous place to be. Because whoever's being blackmailed is going to come for you next."

A sneer. "How was Noelle, Fargo? She's not all that inventive, I'm sorry to say. I tried to teach her but she wasn't the best student I ever had, I'm afraid." The sneer grew bigger. "I did everything I could. She's just a slow learner."

"You've got a dirty mouth. Especially given the fact that she supported you all those years."

"You're one of those who don't like to talk about their conquests, huh?" Rick took another drag of his cigar. "Why don't we compare notes?"

"I'd rather talk about you killing Philly and Bowen."

"You don't know what's going on here, Fargo. You're way, way off. I didn't kill either one of them. I'll admit I kind of took advantage of Philly and Bowen—but killing? I'm a con artist, Fargo."

"You sound proud of it."

He stabbed out his cigar. "What's so noble about working your ass off all day for a few rubles? I give people hope. I set up schemes that make them think they're going to be rich. In that way, I'm like a minister. Except instead of spiritual riches, I offer them financial riches."

"Which they never see."

"Well, whenever I con a lady, I make sure to give her a good deal of pleasure on the side. Now, there can't be anything wrong with that, can there?"

He meant for his smugness to irritate Fargo. It worked.

"What did Philly find out?" Fargo asked.

"I'm afraid that's privileged information. And like I said, I don't have any idea what you're talking about."

"Sure you do. I found some boot prints just inside your door tonight. They're like the ones you left in my room when you followed Philly up there and killed him."

His droll humor left him. "I didn't kill anybody, Fargo. And I'm getting sick of your face."

"You said that already. But I didn't believe you then and I don't believe you now."

"Get the hell out of here."

"What're you going to do if I don't?" Fargo asked. "Scream?"

"That's a damned good idea, in fact," the man said and hurled himself off the far side of the bed. He shouted, "Help! Help!"

In a clapboard house, in the middle of the night, his voice was as strong as a thousand voices. The other people who lived there must have been hardy types because within moments of hearing him, feet slammed to the floor and started pounding to hallways.

Shouts from below as heavy feet slammed up the stairs. Shouts closer by, from the apartment across the hall. Fists pounding on the door.

"You all right in there, Kingsley?"

"Open the door, Kingsley!"

"Maybe somebody should get the sheriff!"

"Don't need no sheriff. I got my Sharps right here!"

Sounded like the house was filled with middle-aged men eager to be part of a posse. And to bag somebody along the way.

Fargo went to the door. Opened it.

Four men with firearms gaped at him. They were all sleepy-faced and night-shirted and bare-footed. They were an unseemly sight.

"Where's Kingsley?" one of them demanded.

Fargo opened the door further, the light from the hallway sconces penetrating the darkness of the room. Kingsley could be seen getting into his street clothes.

"He's right there," Fargo said, waving his hand as a magician would.

"What the hell were you yelling about, Kingsley?" a man said.

"He was trying to kill me," Kingsley said. "This is the infamous Skye Fargo."

"Hey," one of the men said, "I read all about you."

Fargo shook his head. "What we have here, gentlemen, is what you call a constitutional liar. I came up here because I have some pretty strong evidence that Mr. Kingsley himself is a murderer. In fact, a double murderer. In fact, maybe a quadruple murderer. The last part I'm not absolutely sure of. But the first part—being a double murderer—now he looks pretty good for that."

"Who's he supposed to have killed?" the same man said.

"Philly, for starters," Fargo said.

"Philly? Why would he kill Philly?"

"That's what I was trying to find out when he started yelling and all you boys started running here with your guns."

"We don't take shit from nobody is why we came runnin'," the man said. "We're tough guys when we have to be. Every one of us rides posse every chance we get, right, boys?"

As they bragged on, Fargo kept glancing back to see what Rick Kingsley was doing. He was in silhouette against the window, moonlight bathing the glass in gold. He was apparently planning to go out somewhere because he'd just finished putting his boots on and now he was shaping his hat into place.

One of the men said, "This here is private business."

"Sounds like it," said another man.

"You shouldn't ought to yell like that in this kind've situation, Kingsley," said the third man. "He wasn't tryin' to kill you. He was just talking was all."

"What I want to know," said the man who'd spoken first, "is did you kill Philly?"

"Don't be ridiculous," Rick Kingsley said.

Those were his last words here on earth. There were three shots. Rifle shots in quick succession. They shattered the glass, ripped the hat off his head, and put three considerable sized holes in his skull. At just the moment Fargo looked back at him, the top of Kingsley's head was coming off like a furry little animal suddenly taking flight. Except this furry little animal was splattering and spraying blood and brains across the wall.

The four armed men finally got some action. They thundered through the room to the window where they started unloading enough firepower to topple the entire Apache nation.

Fargo left them there. He was already taking the stairs two steps at a time, trying to get outdoors so he could grab the shooter before the man—or woman—got away.

He'd already figured out where the shots had come from, a small mountain of dirt next to an excavation where a house was being built. The site was perfect. There was nobody around as witnesses this time of night. And if you stood on the top of the dirt mound, you had a perfect, clean shot at Kingsley's window.

A shot surprised him. And came close to tearing a good part of his face away. He'd just about drawn even with the mound when somebody fired from a copse of pines up ahead.

He threw himself to the ground and lay as flat and still as possible while two more bullets came close to ripping into him. Then he started rolling, knowing that the third and fourth shots would hit him for sure. The shooter had gotten a bead on him. Rolling away at least forced the shooter to adjust his sights.

A pile of lumber was a good place to take shelter as more bullets started slashing away again. Somebody really wanted Fargo dead. Fargo hunched down then duck-walked to the far end of the lumber. There was a shallow gully that ran up alongside the pines where the shooter was.

Fargo worked his way to the gully and jumped down in it. The bottom was a couple inches deep with water and slippery mud. He inched his way along, knowing that if the shooter spotted him he'd be dead in an instant. There was no place to hide in this gully.

The sweet odor of pine got stronger the closer Fargo got to the shooter. Sweat kept Fargo warm in the chilly night. His legs were getting cramped from haunching down this way.

He stopped.

A dark shape moved around on the far side of the pines. A dark shape with a rifle. The shooter. Fargo made his plan. He could continue to work his way up the gully until he was several yards in back of the shooter. He could sneak up on him and force him to drop his rifle—or die.

12

The only tricky part was moving quietly enough, so that the shooter didn't hear him. The wind had died down. No train wailed in the night. No nocturnal creatures cried out. Damned near perfect silence was the trouble. This was where Fargo's years as a tracker came in handy. He would move with both stealth and speed, coming within three or four yards of where the shooter was. The gully took a sudden turn to the right, and would bring Fargo that close to the shooter.

Fargo readied himself for his brief, quick sweep up the gully.

Suddenly the shooter-shadow turned for no discernible reason and looked in Fargo's direction. They seemed to be staring at each other, though did the shooter really know he was there?

Had Fargo made some noise? Did he give off a scent? Fargo froze in place. And then he heard it, something the shooter must have picked up on first because he was on higher ground. Fargo could hear unseen night animals moving and shifting around as what seemed to be an army of elephants moved sluggishly toward the gully where Fargo hid.

Fargo could see them in the distance. They were still in their night shirts and looked like ghosts. But they had put on their hats. Ghosts with hats. There was a new wrinkle. This would be a second childhood for them. What could be more fun than getting into a battle again? Even if they did have to wear nightshirts instead of uniforms. Tramping through underbrush, puddles of water, mud. Buffaloes could move with more grace and less noise.

"There he is!" a man shouted.

And that's when the fusillade began. The men had mistaken Fargo for the shooter and had now opened up on him. Bullets whizzed, whirred, spanged. And the men cried out exultantly.

Fargo shouted, "You stupid bastards, it's me!"

But apparently they didn't hear him for all the noise their guns were making. Fargo had thrown himself up from the gully, landing in some tall buffalo grass. To avoid being hit, he had to keep rolling. The men kept shooting.

And one by one they started running out of ammunition and needed to reload. And that was when Fargo stood up and waved his hat at them.

"Hey, look!" one of them said. "It's Fargo!"

"Damned right, it's Fargo!" Fargo said.

Could anybody have blamed him for shooting them all right on the spot?

"Hey, I got mud all over the hem of my nightshirt," somebody said.

"Hell," somebody else said, "you should see mine."

When Fargo reached them, the one who did most of the talking said, "Hey, what's the idea of calling us stupid bastards?"

"Yeah," another one said, "we was just tryin' to help you is all."

"Some help," Fargo said. "You chased the shooter away."

"If you didn't want our help, you should've just said so."

"Yeah," said another man. "You don't have to get so shitty about it."

Fargo looked at them and shook his head. "All right. I guess you were just trying to give me a hand."

"Sure, Fargo," one said, "we probably look pretty stupid in our nightshirts and all, but we know what we're doin', don't we, boys?"

"Why don't you go back to sleep?" Fargo said.

"Who could sleep after all this excitement?" said one.

"Damned right," said another. "I'm all ready to shoot somebody."

"Can you think of anybody we should go after, Fargo?"

"Yeah, Fargo, who can we shoot?"

Fargo was about to suggest that the man shoot himself, but that was unkind now, wasn't it? Hooves pounding caught his attention. He was pretty sure who it was. He was also pretty sure that Sheriff Bradshaw would try and tie Fargo to Rick Kingsley's death. He wasn't sure how the lawman would work it around—considering that Fargo had four witnesses who'd say that he didn't have anything at all to do with the shooting—but he knew the lawman would somehow make the charge.

He decided to go face Bradshaw and get it over with.

13

By the time Bradshaw had been on the premises for twenty minutes, more than thirty people had gathered around the house. If it hadn't been so late, if it hadn't been so cold, you might have mistaken the event for a party. A number of people had brought bottles of liquor to stay warm, and there was a lot of laughter considering blood had been spilled just hours earlier.

Fargo stared silently like a child who had misbehaved while Bradshaw shouted questions at him. Bradshaw was a pretty damned inventive inquisitor, Fargo had to give him that.

"You think I don't know what's going on here, Fargo?" Bradshaw was dressed in a blue suit with a few fancy Western touches, a white Stetson, and enough guns to run off a war party. He smelled of whiskey, tobacco, and sleep.

"Then you're ahead of me. Because I sure as hell can't figure it out. Except that somebody was waiting for Kingsley to stand near his window so they could pick him off."

"You think I'm going to buy that bullshit, Fargo?"

"What's bullshit about it? How the hell else could it have happened?"

Bradshaw shook his head, as if he was trying to explain arithmetic to a "slow" person. "It's the middle of the night. He just happens to wake up. And he just happens to walk in front of his window. And his killer just happens to be waiting outside with a rifle."

"Look at where the chamber pot is," Fargo said. "It's

a natural assumption that a man who drinks as much as Kingsley is going to get up and take a leak."

"So the killer waits outside all night?"

"If you really want to kill somebody, that's what you do."

A sour face. "You must really think I'm a dumb bastard, Fargo."

"I don't, Sheriff. There're a lot of things I might accuse you of. But being dumb isn't one of them."

"Well, thank you, Fargo. That was nicely said. And I'm always appreciative of compliments, even from somebody like you. But you know your story for being here is a lie and so do I."

"Like I said, I came here to talk to him."

"Working on who killed Philly."

"Yes."

"Well, right now I'm lookin' for his friend Bowen, and when I find him, I'll know a lot more about who killed Philly."

Bowen. In the pressure of Bradshaw's interrogation, Fargo had forgotten about the dead man back in his room. He almost smiled. If Bradshaw knew about Bowen, the law man would probably have a stroke right on the spot.

"As for Kingsley, here's what happened, Fargo. You came up here, woke him up, got him to stand up and walk to the window. I don't know how you did it, exactly. Maybe you handed him something. However you did it, there he was standing in the middle of the window. A perfect target. And that's when your friend opened fire. Killed him quick and slick."

"And who's my so-called friend?"

"I need to figure it out. But don't worry. I will."

"Withers'll laugh at you."

"Withers laughs at me anyway, Fargo. He thinks I'm this stupid old fart who can't tie his own shoes. He forgets all the towns I cleaned up when I was younger. And I aim to keep this town tame, too. And that means seeing that you meet up with a nice, strong rope. Your luck's run out."

"I don't recall ever laughing at you," Prescott Withers said from the doorway. He was bundled up in a massive great coat that looked as if it weighed a couple hundred pounds. The Easternness of the cumbersome black coat was offset by the frontier touch of his coonskin cap. "I've cursed you, I've threatened you, I've denounced you, Bradshaw. But I've never laughed at you. Only a fool would take you for a fool."

"Two compliments in one night," Bradshaw said. "You two are sure good at buttering somebody up."

"Well, just because I said you weren't a fool doesn't mean that I think you're right about Fargo here. If he was working with an assassin, there had to be a dozen easier ways to move Kingsley into position for getting gunned down."

"This way," Bradshaw said, "he had an alibi. Four men who saw him standing next to Kingsley."

"That I grant you, Sheriff. But again—it's the middle of the night—all sorts of things could've gone wrong."

"Like what?"

"Maybe the other boarders wouldn't have come into Kingsley's room here. So there would've gone Fargo's alibi. And a window gives an assassin a very narrow target. Kingsley could have just taken a step or two backwards and he would've been out of the window. And whatever happened, Fargo would've been in his room at the time of the shooting. And that would've been suspicious, since it was well-known that Fargo and Mr. Kingsley didn't especially like each other."

"So you're saying I shouldn't hold him?"

"I'm saying that you can hold him but then I'll go right from here to Judge Shiner's house and present the case as I see it. And then Judge Shiner will get hold of the county attorney—"

And then something odd happened—odd as Fargo saw it, anyway. Bradshaw just sort of folded his cards. Fargo had been expecting a lot of bluster after Withers finished speaking. But all Bradshaw said, and quietly, almost meekly, was, "Being an attorney, you're not much interested in the truth, Withers." A certain resignation, a certain weariness in his manner now, as if he'd fought a long and noble battle and had lost, at the last minute, and was now too tired to even talk about it anymore. "You know Fargo here's a killer and so do I. And someday, I'll prove it."

As he finished speaking, his deputies wrapped up the body and put it on a stretcher to take downstairs to where the buckboard from the mortuary waited. Bradshaw, without another word, followed the corpse out of the room and down the stairs.

Fargo was finishing up breakfast at the café when Noelle came in. She wore riding pants, knee-high boots, a ruffled white blouse, and a tweed riding jacket. Her hair was pulled back into a chignon. She resembled a lady of the manor. She sat down next to him at the counter, gave her order to the waitress, and said, "You can't seem to stay out of trouble, Skye. Have you thought about leaving town?"

"Withers asked me the same thing. I guess I've thought about it but decided against it. Anyway, I want to stick around and find out what's going on. I thought that's what you wanted me to do."

"I guess we're all getting a little spooked. Even Fiona is. She asked me if I'd buy her out. She wants to go East."

"You don't seem real broken up about Rick."

She smiled. "Do you want some tears? I can do that, you know. Cry when I need to. Make things look good."

"You were married to him."

She thought a long moment, stared into the coffee the waitress had brought her. "Two, three years ago I would've been shattered by him dying. I was in love with him—in lust with him, too. He was quite the man, believe me. But then all his petty con games changed me toward him. You could never believe anything he said. And then when he took up with Fiona—" She bit her lip. "You couldn't trust him with anybody. He had to conquer every woman he met. So I fell out of love with him. Not all at once. But a little bit at a time. One disappointment at a time is a better way to say it." She lifted her head and looked at him. "So I'll shed some tears for him if that'll make you feel better, Skye. But don't ask me to feel sorry for him. He died the way he lived."

"He knew a secret. That's why he died."

"What secret?"

The place was starting to fill up now. Merchants and workingmen mingled in the smoke-choked room. Meat sizzled and cracked and popped on the grill. A slight air of frenzy touched the eyes and mouths of the employees. At this time of morning, most customers were in a hurry. And there were a hell of a lot more customers than there were people to serve them.

Fargo kept the hot, black coffee pouring into his system. He needed the energy. He sensed that if last night had been difficult, today was going to be three or four times worse. It was all coming to a conclusion. But he still had no idea what that would be.

"That's the key to everything," Fargo said. "The secret that got Philly killed. And the secret that killed your husband."

"Please don't call him that, Skye. He was my husband in name only."

"All right. But he and Philly shared a secret. They were blackmailing somebody with it."

"And you don't have any idea what it was?"

"Not exactly. Though I think it has something to do with Suzanna."

Noelle's breakfast came. She had a few forkfuls of her eggs and said, "Suzanna was just a saloon girl. I don't mean to denigrate her, Skye. But she wasn't . . . important. You wanted to hug her and protect her. She was so sweet and vulnerable. But I just can't figure out how she could be involved in some kind of blackmail scheme."

"Maybe there was something about her personally."

"Meaning what?"

"Meaning she came here looking for somebody. That I'm sure of. And whoever she was looking for didn't want to be found."

"Even if that was true, how does it have anything to do with what I hired you for—to find out who's killing the people who are big winners at my casino. And who it was that drove the other two casinos out of business."

"That's what I'm trying to find out."

124

She finished her breakfast and stood up. "I've got a lot of things to do today. I need to get at them."

"You didn't get much sleep last night. Weren't you at the casino late?"

She shrugged. "I don't sleep well, anyway, since this whole thing started." Her face reflected her anger. "I'm going to buy Fiona out. But I'll be damned if I cut and run the way the other two casino people did. They're not going to run me off."

He admired her spirit, but wondered how much longer she could keep operating in the face of all this violence. Plus, there was always the possibility that the people working against her would simply shut down her place the way they had the other two.

"I'll try to help you all I can."

"I appreciate that, Skye. But be careful. Bradshaw really does want to put a rope around your neck."

"Yeah, I kind of noticed that."

He paid for their breakfasts. They walked outside. The fresh new morning air was a relief from all the smoke inside. "I'll probably see you tonight."

"You need some sleep, Skye."

"You're probably right. But I'm like you, I have a hard time sleeping when I'm all worked up about something. I'd just lay there and try and make all these connections."

"Connections?"

"How it all fits. Suzanna, and the trouble you're having at the casino."

"You really think there's a connection?"

Buckboards and a rattling stagecoach passed by in the dirt street.

"Yeah," Fargo said, "now all I have to do is figure out what it is."

14

"Suzanna was very proud of herself," Doris said. "With her limp and all, she always had to prove herself to people. And then bein' an orphan on top of it. And being left-handed. She always said she was 'different' in every way. She wasn't bitter about it, but you could tell it hurt her feelings, the way she was sort of an outsider no matter where she went. Well, you know how you'd feel, Skye. She had a bank account and one of those safety-deposit boxes. She always said it made her feel like a grown up." She yawned and stretched. "I need to get dressed and get back to work," Doris said. "I wish they'd pay me to stay here and make love to you all day, Skye. Now that would be something, wouldn't it?"

"Let me know if you ever find a job like that. I think even I could handle steady employment if it meant you were part of the bargain."

She came over and slid her arms around his waist. "I'll bet you say that to all the girls."

"Only the ones who speak English."

She poked him in the stomach. "I'm never going to see you again after this is over, am I?"

He gave her a deep and affectionate kiss. "We've had a good time together. That's the important thing. I need to get on to California—if I can get out of this town alive."

"You've made a bad enemy, that's for sure."

"Bradshaw, you mean?"

She nodded and moved away. "He does anything he

needs to prove he's right. If he gets it in his mind you're guilty then he'll do anything to throw you in jail. He's sent up a lot of innocent people in this town. At least now—these past five years—the judge has started standing up to him. I think the judge used to be afraid of him, same as everybody else in these parts are."

Fargo got his holster on, tied it down. Walked over to the mirror.

"And they say women are the vain ones," Doris said.

"I've never looked at myself longer than two hours at a time."

She laughed. Shook her head. "Well, time to make some more beds. Where're you headed?"

"Thought I'd get some coffee and think things through a little."

He held the door for her and they went out.

They were halfway down the stairs when Fargo said, "You say she had a safety-deposit box?"

"Uh-huh. And a bank account."

"Anybody know what was in her safety-deposit box?"

"I s'pose not, Skye. She didn't have any kin that anybody knew about. Why?"

"Maybe that safety-deposit box is still there."

"You think there might be something in it?"

"Worth a chance. I think I'll head over there now."

"They close at three. That doesn't leave you much time."

Fargo didn't like bankers on general principle. They were stingy to the poor, and ruthless on collecting. They sided with the rich and powerful as a matter of course. He supposed bankers could get into heaven like everybody else, but Fargo was sure that if heaven had shacks, that's where bankers would be relegated, and while everybody else was drinking expensive wine and eating cherries jubilee such as they served in Frisco, bankers would have to make do with celery and water.

The bank he entered at 2:43 this afternoon was no exception. Apparently, none of the bank employees cottoned much to buckskins. They frowned at Fargo as if he'd dragged a couple of dead skunks inside with him. There were three cages and the tellers in two of them found a reason to close their windows. Whatever he had, they were sure it was catching.

The teller he ended up with looked as if he'd just been sucking on a bag of lemons. He had a thin face that reflected spiritual constipation and a disapproval of most everybody who straggled up to his window. Especially those who straggled up in buckskins.

"Yes, sir. And what is it I can do for you today?"

Fargo was tempted to tell him what he could do for him today, but then he thought better of it. "I'd like to see the president of the bank."

"I'm afraid the president of the bank is out of town."

"Then the vice president."

"I'm afraid the vice president is out dealing with a customer."

"A foreclosure, I assume."

"Yes, as a matter of fact, a foreclosure." He made a clucking sound, his rimless glasses sliding down his small blade of a nose.

"A widow, I hope. And with several starving children."

The clucking sound. "It's very easy to make fun of banks. It's not easy for us, you know. Poor Mister McDougall, every time we have to foreclose he has to work overtime taking care of the paperwork."

"He sounds like an excellent employee."

The sarcasm wasn't lost on the teller. "Exactly what is it I can do for you?"

"Exactly, I need to speak to someone about getting a safety-deposit box opened."

"That would be Mister Woodbury."

"I assume he's out sloughing off like all the rest?"

The teller sucked a few more lemons. If his lips pursed any tighter, somebody'd have to pry them apart with a crowbar. "Do you see that desk over there?"

The bank was large, festooned with piss-elegant mock-Roman posts and woodworking. There were three desks up front on the right side, for customers. The teller cages were on the left. In the back were two large desks, and beyond that an enclosed office that no doubt belonged to the president. To the left of this office was a wall of safety-deposit boxes. And next to that the round pebbled gray face of the vault.

"The desk where the guy is cleaning his nails with his pocket knife?" Fargo asked.

"Mister Woodbury, like all bank employees, believes in keeping sanitary."

"Ah. For a minute there I thought he might be a deadbeat who didn't have anything better to do."

"If you have a question about safety-deposit boxes, Mister Woodbury is the man to ask."

"I just hope he has time to fit me into his schedule."

And with that—unable to take any more of Fargo's abuse—the teller slammed shut the door of his cage, leaving Fargo to walk over to meet Donald R. Woodbury—at least that was the name in gilt on the name bar that sat in the exact center of the desk. Woodbury had just snapped his pocket knife shut and was now sorting through some papers. He also kept glancing at the big clock on the wall. Here was obviously a dedicated servant of the bank and its public.

"The teller over there sent me over here," Fargo said.

"You couldn't come back tomorrow, could you?" Woodbury said.

"Are you open on Saturday?"

"Oh. I forgot tomorrow is Saturday."

"So I'd really like to do this now, Mister Woodbury."

"And just what would that consist of, what you want to do now?"

Fargo told him about the safety-deposit box and wanting to open it.

"Are you related to her?"

"No."

"Did you know her well?"

"No."

"Well, then how could I open her box for you?"

"I'm trying to find out who killed her, Mister Woodbury."

"She killed herself."

"I don't think that's true, Mister Woodbury."

"Well, Sheriff Bradshaw certainly seems to think it's true," Woodbury said, casting an anxious glance at the clock.

"I don't want to take anything with me, Mister Woodbury. What I was hoping was that you'd open the box and let me see what's in there."

Woodbury sat back in his chair and looked Fargo up and down. "You know what you look like to me in those buckskins of yours?"

"No, I guess I don't."

"Standing there in those buckskins of yours, and intimating that our beloved sheriff doesn't know the difference between suicide and murder—you look like a troublemaker to me."

"I see."

He cast another furtive glance at the clock. "And do you know what Donald R. Woodbury says to troublemakers?"

"I guess I don't."

"Donald R. Woodbury says 'Good day, sir' and walks right out the door at the appointed time of his departure."

Which is just what Donald R. Woodbury proceeded to do. Stacked the papers he'd been looking through, closed his desk drawers, picked up his derby from a nearby hat rack, grabbed a small valise and said, "Good day, sir."

The three tellers were back at their windows for the closing three minutes of the day. Donald R. Woodbury said good bye to each of them. They smirked back at him. They'd heard how he wiggled his way out of staying past three o'clock. They knew envy, they knew respect. Not even the hand of fate could inhibit Donald R. Woodbury. He was one of those employees who would always be out that door no later than 3:01 and not a forest fire, not a dragon, not a lost army of Amazon headhunters could slow him down.

Fargo walked over to the lemon-sucker at the teller window. "Is there anybody I could speak to now, since Donald R. Woodbury just left?"

"I'm afraid not."

"And why would that be?"

"A, because the bank day is over. And, B, because Mr. Woodbury is the only one familiar with the safety-deposit boxes. He has everything in his desk."

But by then, Fargo didn't much care what the lemon-sucker said. Because by divulging where all the safety-deposit records were kept, Fargo already knew what he needed to do. Tonight, he would break into the bank.

15

He spent the rest of the afternoon making sure that everybody would show up tonight at Fiona's place for the get-together she didn't yet know she was having.

He paid his last visit to Fiona herself. She greeted him at the door in her wheelchair. "Oh," she said, "it's you." After he closed the doors, she got up out of her chair and said, "Would you like a glass of beer?"

"That'd be great."

While she was getting their beers, Fargo sat in her wheelchair and tooled around the large living room with the parquet floor.

When she came back from the kitchen, Fargo said, "A fella could get goin' pretty fast in one of these things."

She laughed. "I'm so glad you're so sensitive to the needs of the disadvantaged."

He stayed in the chair, sipping his beer. "At least I don't fake being crippled."

"I guess that's a point. What I'm doing to my sister is pretty cruel. But the bitch deserves it."

"I'd sure hate to get on the wrong side of either one of you."

"A big, bad man like you afraid of two slight little girls?"

"Slight little girls?" Fargo grinned. "You really expect me to believe that's how you see yourselves? You could destroy any man in this town if you put your mind to it."

"Are you trying to implicate me in something, Skye?"

"Maybe," he said, with no humor at all.

"Oh," she said. She sounded both shocked and angry. "Well, that's very nice."

"That's why I'm having a little get-together here tonight."

"What're you talking about?"

"I've asked a few people over. I'm pretty sure that at least one of them is behind all these killings."

"I take it I'm one of the ones you think might be guilty?"

"It's at least a possibility."

"I really appreciate you asking me if these people could come over."

Fargo grinned. "I just felt that a sensitive woman confined to a wheelchair would be happy to help an old friend like me out."

"You're really a bastard, you know that?"

"All I care about is finding the killer. Or killers."

"You think there might be more than one?"

"I sure can't rule it out at this point."

She'd been sitting on a love seat. Now she stood up and walked over to lean against the stone fireplace. "Reverend Amis is still the most likely one in my opinion."

"I'm hoping he shows up. I saw one of his flock in town and had the man deliver a handwritten invitation."

"The house isn't terribly clean. It's the maid's day off."

Fargo got up from the wheelchair. "I doubt they'll be noticing that kind of thing. They'll be a lot more concerned about why I wanted them here." He handed her his empty beer glass. "I'll see you later tonight. Thanks for the beer."

She didn't see him to the door.

Just before supper time, Fargo returned to his hotel room. Bowen was still flung across the chair where Fargo had put him.

The corpse was becoming more corpse-like. He was almost too stiff and awkward to stuff into the closet. There wasn't yet any way to get him out of this room. Fargo had to catch the real killer tonight or he'd have

133

to get Bradshaw up here and show him another corpse. By then the stench would be unbearable. It wasn't all that pleasant now. Fargo tried several times to get Bowen's eyes closed. Nothing worked. Bowen just stared straight ahead.

Fargo got the closet door closed just in time for the knock on the door.

There stood fetching Doris, more fetching than usual.

She fluttered her feather duster at him. "I thought I'd wait till you got back to clean your room. Give me a good excuse to see you."

"You don't need an excuse to see me."

"I'm not too sure about that, Fargo. I get the sense that I scare you a little bit." She came into the room. "What's that smell?"

"What smell?" Bowen was starting to get rancid.

"You really don't smell it?"

"Smell what?"

"God, it's awful." But then she slid her arms around his waist and seemed to forget the odor.

"Do all customers get this kind of treatment?" he said.

"Only ones I dream about."

Fargo backed away, took off his shirt and started washing his chest and underarms. "You know much about Reverend Amis?"

"Just that he's got a crazy son."

"You ever know him to try and get rich?"

"Amis? Not that I know of. I think if you gave him the choice between a pot of gold and denouncing somebody from his pulpit, he'd choose the pulpit. Why?"

"Fiona seems to think he's behind these murders."

"What would he get out of them?"

"That's what I was wondering. He doesn't strike me as the kind."

"Fiona just hates him because he made her life so miserable. Always having those pickets out in front of the casino."

He watched Doris in the bureau mirror. She reminded him of a cat; clean, efficient, self-sufficient. She moved from fluffing the pillow on the bed to dusting the window frame to straightening the chair in an unbroken glide. The feather duster was like an extension of her arm.

"You need some fresh water," she said. And snatched the basin from beneath his hands. She walked out the door. He smiled to himself. She was displaying her many charms and homemaking gifts for him. He almost felt guilty for being unable to take up her offer to pursue their relationship further. But he had many miles to travel before he reached that sweet little cottage by the fast, clean creek where the big collie played with all the tykes. He had many, many miles to travel before that came to pass.

She bustled back in with a basin of fresh water. "So are you going to take me to the café for supper?"

"I reckon I could be talked into that."

She studied him. "Am I pushing too hard? I do that sometimes. Most of the time I'm not even aware of it."

"A little bit, maybe. But you're a very likable gal."

They had moved toward each other in the middle of the room, just about to embrace when the knock came on the closed door.

She slid her arms around him, nuzzling her breasts against his chest. She whispered, "We could always pretend we're not here."

He gave her a quick kiss and went to the door. The desk clerk stood there. "We're getting crowded with drummers this weekend, Mr. Fargo. Will you be staying a few more days?"

"Far as I know."

The clerk didn't look unduly happy. "Your stay hasn't been exactly quiet."

"Through no fault of my own."

"Be that as it may—"

"Oh, Earl, why don't you tell Mister Fargo the truth?"

Earl blushed. "I'm sure I don't know what you're talking about."

"Earl has asked me out once a week since he started working here," Doris said. "And every time I get interested in one of our guests, Earl tries to run them off."

Earl sniffed. He sniffed the way a hunting dog would.

His head lifted, his nostrils quivered, his eye darted about the room. "What's that smell?"

"What smell?" Fargo said, too quickly.

Doris must have seen the panic in Fargo's eyes. She picked up on the moment quickly. "What smell? I don't smell anything."

"You don't smell anything?" Earl said.

"No."

Fargo took the edge of the door in his right hand and began to close it on Earl. But Earl put a surprisingly manful hand on the door, too.

"What's going on in here?" Earl demanded.

"Earl, shouldn't you be downstairs at the desk?" Doris said, sweetly enough. "This is our busy time of night."

But Earl was resolute. "Something smells terrible. And I demand to know what it is."

Fargo sighed. "Well, I didn't want to tell you, Earl. But I guess I don't have any choice, do I?"

"Just tell me what it is and skip the malarkey."

"It's you, Earl," Fargo said deadpan. "Several guests have mentioned it, in fact. They think you need a bath as soon as possible."

"You're just so hilarious, aren't you, Fargo?" Earl said primly. Then he surprised everybody, probably including himself, by producing from somewhere at the back of his trousers, a derringer. "Don't make any mistake, Fargo. This could kill you."

It probably couldn't, Fargo thought. But it could put some hurt on me.

Earl had just started to walk into the room when somebody shouted up the stairs, "Hey! Can we get some help down here?"

"I told you, Earl," Doris said.

Earl was back to sniffing, doggie-style. "It smells like rotted meat."

"Or," Fargo said cordially, "somebody who hasn't rubbed up against a bathtub in a couple of months."

"You're so hilarious, Fargo."

"You mentioned that already, Earl," Fargo said.

"Hey!" The shouter sounded angrier. "Where the hell's the desk clerk in this place?"

"You'd better get down there, Earl," Doris said.

Earl fumed. "Don't you two worry. I'll be back."

"Good ole reliable Earl," Fargo said to Doris. "He'll be back."

"Good ole Earl," Doris said.

Earl slipped the derringer back into its secret hiding place, sniffed some more, fumed some more, and then stalked out of the room without another word.

Doris closed the door. Then she turned to Fargo. "You have a body in here, don't you, Skye?"

"You know a man named Bowen?"

"Sure. A friend of Philly's."

"That's who's in there."

The knock on the door startled them both. But the visitor knocked only as a formality. He pushed the door inward and stood there on the threshold looking like a villain on the cover of a dime novel. Well, except for the watery eyes and overbite and weak chin and pot belly.

"That's a good way to get shot, Earl," Fargo said.

"I got somebody to cover the desk for me," Earl said. "Now, I want you to open that door for me."

"Earl, you're a real pain in the ass, you know that?" Doris said. "There's nothing in that closet except Skye's clothes."

"Open it," Earl said.

"Earl," Doris said.

"Open it now," Earl said.

Fargo took a deep breath. One way or another good ole Earl here was going to find the corpse Fargo had stashed in the closet. "Might as well open it," Fargo said.

So she opened it.

The odor was still there, that was for sure. But the body was gone. The closet was innocent of everything but Fargo's corpse-stenched clothes.

16

He went out into the night. The bank was two blocks to the north, well out of the heavy traffic of the area where the casino and the saloons were. That would be a help.

He huddled inside his sheepskin—the night wind almost bitter—and made his way around back of the hotel. Best to take alleys all the way to the bank. The fewer people who saw him, the better.

Cats, rats, and dogs observed his passage down the rutted alleys that gleamed with frost on this moonful cold night. The wind even robbed all the garbage behind the café of its usual odor. In the gloom a drunk stirred and said something that probably not even he could understand in sober light of day.

The rear of the bank was dark, as he'd expected. What he hadn't expected was a night deputy to be here. Making his rounds, apparently. Rattling the doorknob, angling his head so that he could peer inside around the edge of the drawn shade.

Fargo hid behind a stack of boxes twenty yards down the alley. The deputy took his time, rolling himself a smoke, using up three matches before he could get the thing going. Then he huddled deep into his dark jacket and started to step down off the rear steps of the bank.

The deputy paused. Had he seen Fargo? Fargo tried to shrink himself down to kid-size behind those boxes. If he got caught now, he'd never be able to find the killer. He eased his Colt from his holster, ready if he needed to be.

The deputy came off the steps. He was heavy enough

to rock the entire wooden structure of the stairs. He walked out into the alley and gazed down it. Did he know that Fargo was here and was just playing games? No, if he did, he would have drawn his gun by now. Would he walk down here and look around? He sure was taking his time surveying the alley. Fargo got the sense that the deputy was debating what to do next. The man drew on his cigarette thoughtfully and continued to stare into the gloom.

Then he moved. Since Fargo couldn't read minds, he had no idea why the deputy just up and turned around and headed back to the mouth of the alley.

Fargo felt a moment of relief. But the feeling was short-lived. Fargo's devious mind began to see a possible reason for the deputy suddenly exiting this way. What if the man was setting a trap? Maybe he'd spotted Fargo. Maybe now what he wanted was for Fargo to somehow get inside the bank. Then Bradshaw would have something definite and incontrovertible to charge him with. Bank robbery. Boy, wouldn't Bradshaw love that. And Fargo would be no nearer to finding the killer.

But what other choice did Fargo have than to move to the bank and get inside and look for the safety-deposit box?

Fargo eased himself out from behind the boxes. A tom cat yowled at him.

Fargo felt self-conscious now. As if human eyes were peering at him, watching. The deputy? Was the deputy hiding somewhere watching him? He'd be having a good laugh if he was. Observing Fargo sneaking down the alley to the back door. Moving up the rear bank steps with great stealth. Constantly turning around to see if anybody was watching him.

Oh, the deputy would be getting a great laugh out of it, no doubt.

But again—what choice did he have?

He examined the padlock. Took out his knife. Inserted the tip into the lock mechanism. This lock would be a problem. It was more sophisticated—as befitted a bank—than the ones he usually encountered. There was a chance that there would be a bell of some kind wired to the rear of the door so that when it opened the clanging would be loud and clear in the night. Anybody in the vicinity would know that the bank was being robbed.

There was a rectangular window above the door. One of the many skills Fargo had developed as a tracker was the ability to scale just about any surface. He jumped up, grabbing the bottom of the window. He next put his foot on the doorknob to give himself better purchase. This gave him enough of a perch to examine the window closely. It was puttied in place, meaning that he could knock the window out with the help of his knife. The big problem here was that it would take some time to loosen enough putty to push the window out.

He had just set to work when he heard the footsteps. With the earth this frost-hardened, the footsteps were loud in the narrow confines of the alley.

And then the singing started.

Fargo's first instinct had told him that the deputy had returned. But it was unlikely the deputy would return singing a few tattered bars of a melancholy popular song of the day. Not unless they were teaching folks some damned strange things at deppity school these days.

The man was obviously a drunk.

Fargo went back to work. At the turtle pace the drunk was moving, it would be several minutes before he reached Fargo and the door.

The putty proved more formidable than Fargo had imagined. What he had to do now was smash the window with his fist, find the window lock, unlatch it, and crawl inside. But he couldn't do this till the drunk passed.

The man had almost drawn abreast of Fargo now. He continued to sing. He not only had a terrible voice, he didn't know the lyrics very well, either. The song was one Fargo knew well, and liked. He had the irrational urge to shout down and set him straight. But that probably wasn't a very good idea now, was it?

The man was doing a stage act. He wiggled, he waggled, he wobbled. The first thing he did within Fargo's sight was accidentally knock his derby off his head and then stoop over and try to pick it up. He nearly went over face first. But somehow he managed to right himself and continue to proceed down the alley.

For five or six more steps, anyway. He came to an abrupt stop and turned back suddenly. His head was revolving around as if it was on ball bearings. But finally it sat still and the drunk focused his eyes on the odd sight of a man in buckskins standing on the back door of the bank with a brick in hand.

The image quickly faded to black as Skye reluctantly threw the brick down, clocking the inebriated fellow across the top of his head and knocking him unconscious.

While it wasn't Fargo's favorite action, as the man had done nothing wrong, considering the circumstances he knew he had no other choice.

Fargo turned his attention back to the task at hand. He took off his hat, shoved his fist inside of it, and smashed out one of three panes as delicately as he could. The sound of falling glass was loud for only a moment. Then the night sounds—winds, saloons, a train—covered any noise Fargo made.

He reached inside, found the latch, and pushed the window open. The squeeze was tighter than he'd anticipated. He had a brief fear of getting trapped within the window frame. He could hear Bradshaw laughing now. But he set to moving himself side to side with enough facility to wangle himself through all the way to the backs of his thighs. The rest was simple. He dropped headfirst to the floor, breaking his fall with splayed hands, the way gymnasts did in circus acts.

Moonlight limned a dozen shapes, among them desks, tellers' cages, a coat stand, and a reception area where customers could sit while waiting to see the more prestigious members of the bank staff. Somebody had applied heavy doses of furniture polish this evening. The air was sweet and heavy and not unpleasant with the aroma.

He let himself enjoy the feeling of being inside the bank all by himself. A burglar's dream. All that money. Too bad he wasn't inclined to crime.

Then he got to work. Woodbury's desk drawers were a chaos of letters and envelopes and ledgers and odd sheets of papers that had been shoved inside in a variety of ways. Fargo sat in Woodbury's chair and went through the drawers carefully. He needed two things, a list of safety-deposit boxes and who they belonged to, and the keys to that box. Normally, the bank kept one and the customer kept one. But he was hoping that Suzanna's had been returned.

He found what he needed, of course, in the very last drawer. That was always the way, wasn't it? Wouldn't a feller be smart to take his starting point and reverse it, start last to first? Ah, but what the hell, he'd found the box number and the keys.

He crept across the floor to the shadowy area where the safety-deposit boxes lined the wall. He wanted Box 27.

The rest was easy. He slid the box out and took it over to the table where box customers could do their business in private.

The box was long and shallow. He found a small letter with the words "To Whom It May Concern" written in a careful and feminine hand on the front. It was the sole item in the box.

He took the letter over to a long window aglow with moonlight. He'd be able to read it there.

Then he heard heavy boots crunching through glass on the back steps. And the door opening. And a voice saying: "Mooney, what the hell happened to you?"

The voice of the deputy, no doubt. Making his rounds. Coming around to find out if anything was amiss. With the window above the rear door broken, shards of glass on the steps, and good ole off-key Mooney passed out in a bundle below, the whole situation was about to be offically out of control. Fargo had what he wanted. Now he needed to get out of here. There was probably a bell alarm on the front door. That meant the only option was back the way he came. Better to deal with one deputy over a whole posse.

Mooney started to come around. He tried talking but none of the words were quite articulated.

Fargo pulled his Colt and started climbing his way up the wall and out of the window. Mooney saw him first. He became frog-eyed and frantic, as Fargo sat poised above the alley, ready to jump.

But it was already too late as Fargo came crashing down on the unsuspecting deputy.

Another voice said, "What the hell's goin' on in here?"

Ken Stalling, the massive deputy Fargo had battled with, stood blocking the alley's entrance. His gun was drawn.

Fargo moved quickly. He grabbed the other deputy, spun him around, got an arm around his throat hostage-style. "I don't want to hurt anybody so just let me walk on out of here."

"Put your gun down, Fargo," Stalling said.

"You know I'm not gonna do that," Fargo said.

"You done enough stuff tonight for Bradshaw to hang you already. You kill a deputy, Bradshaw won't even bother with a trial. Now put that gun down."

Mooney erupted with another bombardment of incomprehensible words.

"If you want to shoot somebody, shoot him," Fargo said, nodding to Mooney.

"Always with the smart remarks, Fargo," Stalling said. "Think you're some kind of dime novel hero. Well, you ain't. You're just another gunny all them pansy journalists write lies about to sell their rags. You're not jack shit to me and you ain't goin' nowhere, you understand?"

Fargo heard a faint damp sound and realized that his hostage had just wet his pants.

"There's no place to run, Fargo," Stalling said. "You might as well drop your gun. Because in a minute or two I'm goin' to start firin'."

"You'll kill him!"

"He knew what he was in for when he signed on. Always over to the Ruby Rooster runnin' his mouth about what a tough boy he is, here's where he gets to own up to it."

Fargo knew that Stalling wasn't bluffing. He really would shoot the kid if he needed to. Probably shoot to kill, just for the pleasure of it. Who'd be able to challenge him that he'd done it on purpose?

Fargo considered his chances. Slim and none, basically.

That was when Fargo made his move. He fired two shots into Stalling's gun hand. The deputy cried out, spun around, slammed into the wall. Fargo pushed his hostage away and went and grabbed the guns belonging to the lawmen. Even if they came after him, they wouldn't have any firearms. He stuck the guns in his belt.

17

Fiona's downstairs windows lanced lamplight onto the lawn. Through the window, Fargo could see Withers, Bradshaw, and Noelle and Fiona. Each held a drink. None looked especially happy.

Fargo had taken the time to read the letter he'd found in Suzanna's safety deposit box. It told him more than he could have hoped for.

He ground-tied his stallion and went to the front door and knocked. Noelle was there in moments. "I'm not thrilled with this, Skye. Not at all."

"I didn't expect you to be," Fargo said as he stepped into the vestibule. He saw the others collected by the French doors that opened upon the parlor. "Any of you."

"I don't know what you think you're doing, Fargo," Bradshaw said. "But I have to admit you made me curious."

"Me, too," said the aged lawyer Withers. "I mostly came for the free drinks." He grinned like a kid.

"I'm not very happy about Bradshaw being in my house," Fiona said from her wheelchair, glowering at the lawman.

"Let's go into the parlor," Fargo said.

Noelle pushed Fiona's wheelchair. Fargo noted that she didn't do a delicate job of it, either. She shoved it jerkily along. Fiona said, "Do you have to be so rough?"

"Oh, we wouldn't want poor Fiona to suffer any more than she has to, would we now?"

"Noelle!" Withers snapped. "That's a terrible thing for you to say to your sister!"

Noelle took it easy the rest of the way into the parlor.

"Looks like we're ready for a seance," Fiona said.

"Or a poker game," Fargo said.

A table and five chairs. A lantern on a small table beneath a window. A crystal ball or a deck of cards would have done nicely. Instead, everybody got themselves seated around the table. Noelle freshened up their drinks. Withers looked excited about getting another free drink. Even Bradshaw seemed looser than normal. He undercut this impression by saying, "You know, Fargo, I'm going to arrest you as soon as this little road show of yours is over."

"For what?"

"Don't worry," the lawman said. "I'll think of something."

Withers actually giggled. "I didn't think I'd ever live long enough to hear Bradshaw here say something witty. But by damn, he did."

"Can we get started, Fargo?" Noelle said. "I have to get back to the casino."

"Get a few more of your customers shot?" Bradshaw said.

"I thought you said he was witty," Noelle said to Withers.

Fiona said, "Please, Skye. Start."

Fargo took the envelope from inside his buckskin shirt and laid it on the table. "I'm going to give you a reason to arrest me, Bradshaw."

"Oh?"

"I broke into the bank tonight and took this letter from Suzanna's safety deposit box."

"You're right, Fargo," Bradshaw said. "Consider yourself under arrest."

Fargo waved the letter around the way a magician would wave a prop just before he was about to dazzle people with it. A scarf becomes a pigeon; an Ace of Hearts vanishes. In this case, the prop would name a killer.

"The letter tells us two things," Fargo said.

"What if we don't believe you that you actually took

this from Suzanna's safety-deposit box?" Withers said. "What if it's a forgery?"

"Fiona and Noelle knew her well. You've seen her write things, haven't you?"

They both nodded.

"Then they'll be able to verify that this is a letter that Suzanna wrote."

"Why would she put it in a safety-deposit box?" Bradshaw said.

"Because she obviously suspected that somebody was going to kill her."

"Did she know who that was?" Fiona said.

"Yes." Fargo hesitated. "But the letter answers another question, too."

"What question?" Noelle said.

"The question of why Suzanna came to Cumberland in the first place. She discovered the killer by accident. Her real concern was seeking vengeance against somebody who'd wronged her."

He glanced around the table at each of them. Each was a practiced liar. You had to be to be a lawman, so as to not divulge your real feelings and give away your suspicions. You had to be a practiced liar to run a casino, to convince people that they really did have a chance of beating the house. You had to be to be a lawyer; lies frequently won juries over.

"So why did she come here?" Withers said.

Fargo said, "To kill her father."

"What're you talking about, Skye?" Fiona demanded. "Her father lived in Cumberland?"

"Lived—and still does. As a matter of fact, he's with us here now at the table."

One surprise followed another. First, Fargo's claim that Suzanna's father was here in their midst. And second, Fiona bringing a six-shooter up from beneath the table and pointing it at Fargo—and then pushing her wheelchair back from the table and standing up. He kicked backward, and the chair wheeled backward several screeching feet.

"She can walk!" Withers said.

"You bitch!" Noelle snapped. "You've been faking all this time?"

147

Fiona smiled. "Yes, but I certainly appreciate all the help you gave me as an invalid."

Withers said, "Fiona's behind all the killings?"

Fargo nodded. "She figured if she could close down every casino in town, then she and her partner could set up their own and do very well."

Bradshaw stood up now, his gun drawn. "Give me your gun, Fargo. And right now."

"Are you planing to kill all three of us?" Fargo said. "To add to Philly and Bowen and the others? By the way, Bowen really stunk up my room."

"Your gun, Fargo," Bradshaw said. "Or I'll kill you right now. It's up to you." He leveled his Colt right at Fargo's face.

"So Bradshaw is Fiona's partner?" Withers said.

"Yes, and he was Suzanna's father. Her mother was a saloon girl in one of the towns he cleaned up. When she was sixteen, Suzanna wanted to marry a nineteen-year-old kid she insisted was a decent lad who'd gotten into a few minor scrapes with the law. But her father—who visited her once a year in Utah—saw things differently. He saw the boy as a bad one. And when he couldn't talk her out of the marriage, he forced the boy into a gunfight and killed him. Suzanna never forgave him."

"Her mother told me to kill that boy," Bradshaw said. "She knew what kind of gutter trash he was going to turn into."

"That's the thing, Bradshaw," Fargo said. "There was no way you could predict he was going to turn into trash. You just assumed he would. So you killed him."

"Did Suzanna know Bradshaw and Fiona were hooked up together?" Noelle said.

"Yes," Fargo said. "But like I said, she learned it by accident. She followed Bradshaw around, trying to see where he was vulnerable. And one night she saw Bradshaw and Fiona together and then followed Bradshaw when he killed one of the casino customers. She enjoyed working as a saloon girl, by the way, Bradshaw. She knew how much you hated her for it. And then she decided to have some fun with you. She started to sweat you, told you she was going to tell everybody what you and Fiona were up to. So you killed her. You faked her suicide. And then Philly stole some old papers out of your desk and showed them to Bowen and Rick. And one by one you killed them, too. For a while everything looked like it was going to be all right."

"But it didn't turn out that way, did it?" Doris said, coming into the parlor.

Fargo had made sure to leave the door open a crack. Doris had agreed to hide outside the house and listen and at the appropriate time walk in with her shotgun.

"Put it down easy, Bradshaw," Doris said. "You, too, Fiona."

"You can't kill us both," Bradshaw said.

"Well, in that case," Doris smiled. "Why don't I start with you, Sheriff? I never thought you were worth a spit, anyway. Now you put that gun of yours down before I open up that gut of yours."

Bradshaw clearly realized that his six-shooter couldn't do to her what her shotgun could do to him. He tossed his gun on the table so hard it was obvious he hoped the weapon would misfire and kill somebody, preferably Fargo, which is where the barrel pointed. But no such luck.

Fargo grabbed his own gun. "Now you, Fiona."

"What if I don't?"

"Then I'll hand this gun to your sister," Fargo said, "and I'm sure she'll do me the honor of shooting you herself."

"You bitch," Noelle said. "Damned right I'll kill you."

Fiona made a face that almost did the impossible—made her ugly—then set her weapon down on the table. There was a moment there when both Fargo and Doris felt themselves relaxing, but that was short-lived. Just then Bradshaw grabbed the lantern on the small table by the window and hurled it at Doris.

Flames covered the upper part of her body instantly. Her cry was as frightened and sorrowful as anything Fargo had ever heard. His entire attention was given to her.

The oil from the lamp soon doused her hips and legs, and fire erupted there, too. She was completely encased in licking, murderous flames.

Fargo dove for her, yanking a curtain down from its rod, wrapping the curtain around her and throwing her to the floor. The first thing was to get the fire out. As she slipped into unconsciousness, her screams faltered.

He rocked her from side to side, feeling the flames die beneath his gentle touch. He could see a portion of her face between the folds of the curtain. Her skin was a raw, red, charred mask; her eyes huge and white, otherworldly.

When the rage came, he could not control it. He jumped to his feet.

Withers held a gun on Fiona. Noelle stood looking down in horror at Doris. Her hands covered her face.

"I'm going after Bradshaw," Fargo said. "Hold Fiona till I get back."

"I just don't know how you could've done such a thing," Withers said wearily to Fiona.

Fiona just glared at him.

18

Ground fog was setting in. It would be thicker as Fargo got out of town. He rode hard to the center of Cumberland and asked the first man he saw on the street, "You see Bradshaw?"

"Few minutes ago, I did," the man said. "He was headed out the stage road. Ridin' hard. Figured he was chasin' somebody."

Fargo thanked the man and spurred his horse. Bradshaw knew this section of Oregon Territory much better than Fargo did. He wouldn't have any trouble finding places to hide. In the morning he'd likely make his escape. Fargo needed to move fast and hard.

By the time he reached the town limits, fog touched his stirrups. The moon was bright, though, so he didn't have any trouble seeing the roadside where Bradshaw might be hiding with a rifle. Maybe instead of running away from Fargo, he had decided to ambush him.

This was the road Fargo had taken when he traveled to Reverend Amis's place. The trees and rocks held a certain familiarity for him. He just hoped his Ovaro didn't stumble on a rock that neither of them could see coming.

Fargo rode a fast mile with the reins in his right hand and his rifle in the other. If Bradshaw did open fire, Fargo wanted to retaliate in kind. With a rifle.

The night air was cold; the fog was like skeletal fingers on his face.

The sudden sound of the horse's screams chilled him. He instantly pictured what had happened. Bradshaw was maybe an eighth of a mile ahead of him. His mount had stumbled into a rut or hole. The animal's misery was almost intolerable to hear. Bradshaw had enough humanity in him to put the poor horse away. The single gunshot was lonely and sad in the night.

Fargo was inches from the dead horse moments later. He saw Bradshaw headed for the timber.

The lawman turned and yelled, "You ruined my life, Fargo, you know that? You and my daughter. I got just a few years left anyway. I did a lot of good for a lot of towns and a lot of people. I deserve to pass out my time with a little money. I never stole nothing till now, Fargo. Not a penny."

A small field separated the men. Fargo dropped from his horse and started across the fog-bound grass. Like most bad men, Bradshaw spoke with great self-justification and self-pity. They were good men, most bad men would tell you, if you just looked at them a certain way.

Bradshaw's lies and distortions sickened him. "How about the girl you set on fire back there? I'll never forget her screams, Bradshaw, not as long as I live."

"You stay where you are, Fargo," Bradshaw shouted across the ever-narrowing plot of grass that separated them. "You stay where you are or I'll shoot you down. And that's a promise."

But Fargo was no longer listening to Bradshaw. All he could hear was Doris' screams. He opened fire, his first bullet ripping into Bradshaw's shoulder. The force of the shot knocked Bradshaw into the forest. He squeezed off two shots of his own but apparently Fargo's bullet had hit his shooting arm because the shots were wild.

Fargo kept coming. All he could think of was the horrific sight of poor Doris's face. All he could think of was his need to know that Bradshaw was dead.

By this point, Fargo himself had reached the timber. He just kept moving straight forward. His finger on the trigger of his rifle.

Bradshaw shouted, "You're not gonna get me, Fargo! I'm gonna surprise you! You wait and see!"

He could hear Bradshaw in the woods. He sounded

like some huge, crazed animal. Low-hanging branches snapped off. Bushes and foliage rattled loud as drums. Night animals scurried out of Bradshaw's way.

Bradshaw cried out. He must have fallen into some kind of hole. There was a furious shaking of foliage and pine branches as the big man apparently righted himself and set off again. He left a thousand curses on the dark, dank air.

A few minutes later, Fargo sensed that he was drawing much nearer to Bradshaw. A curious hissing sound reached Fargo's ears, a sound he recognized at once.

He wondered if Bradshaw recognized it. Fargo's memory supplied images from a few days past when he had seen the huge footprints of the puma along the road. And then came the low rumble that reminded Fargo of whose domain this section of timber really was. The murderous mountain lion. Goldie, as the locals sardonically called the killer.

Ahead of him now he saw a small, rectangular clearing in the middle of the timberland. Bradshaw stood in the center of it, the puma, majestic in the size and muscled dominance of its body, crouching before him. The puma was the least theatrical of major predators. No intimidating sounds before it struck its victim. It desired only one thing and that was the death and utter evisceration of its prey.

Bradshaw fired at it, but again, since it was not his shooting arm, the shots went wild. "Help me, Fargo! Help me!" he screamed.

Fargo had to clear his head of Doris's screams before he could address Bradshaw. Fargo raised his rifle. He couldn't let the bastard die this way.

But by the time Fargo sighted his rifle and pumped two bullets into the beast's massive torso, Bradshaw's face was already exploding into blood and bone that shone in the merciless moonlight.

The beast lived just long enough to tear out Bradshaw's heart and stomach and then, with two more of Fargo's shots blowing away a good share of its skull, it collapsed on what was left of the lawman.

Fargo put two more rounds into the puma. And then a vast, somber silence filled the clearing. For a windless moment not even the nocturnal creatures of slither and shadow could be heard. There was just the silence.

Soon after, Fargo made his way back to his horse and headed back for town.

Fargo stayed around for Doris's funeral two days later. The ceremony was brief and simple, befitting the sweet, unpretentious young woman.

After the burial, on the grassy hillside where Doris's tombstone resided, Noelle and Withers came up to him.

"Sure wish you'd reconsider that offer of ours," Withers said. "You'd make a mighty good sheriff."

"Afraid I wouldn't," Fargo said. "Sometimes I'd cut a lot of corners going after the bad guys. I probably'd end up a lot like Bradshaw used to be. I've seen what happens to town tamers. They start thinking they're God. And then they start acting like the people they're chasing after."

"Then you could work for me," Noelle said. "With Fiona heading for prison the rest of her life, I'd sure like a partner."

Fargo took her in his arms and hugged her. "You'll find a good one. And it probably won't take as long as you think."

He gave them a jaunty little salute and then walked over to his horse. He'd be back on the trail soon enough. California sounded like as good a destination as any.

The Trailsman rode on.

appearing out of nowhere in these parts, and outlaws could be lurking in those gullies and washes, too. A pilgrim who was not careful was a pilgrim who might soon be dead.

Skye Fargo was no pilgrim. He was the Trailsman.

He nudged the black-and-white pinto forward into an easy lope that carried man and horse across the prairie at a ground-eating pace. The Platte River was off to Fargo's right, curving southeastward. Ahead of him, running down from the north, was the Elkhorn. Farther east lay the relatively new city of Omaha, which was just across the Missouri River from Council Bluffs, Iowa. For twenty years or so, Council Bluffs had been one of the jumping-off places for wagon trains full of immigrants bound for what they hoped would be paradise. When news of gold strikes in Colorado arrived, the city fathers of Council Bluffs had come up with the idea of establishing a new town on the western bank of the Missouri to better serve the thousands of new immigrants bound for the gold mines. In the half-dozen years since then, Council Bluffs had been far outstripped by Omaha as an outfitting point for wagon trains. Now the territorial capital of Nebraska, Omaha was quite a booming place.

Fargo had no doubt he would be able to find the things he was looking for there: a game of cards; a drink of whiskey; a real bed; and, most importantly, a warm, willing woman to share it with him.

He had spent the past month guiding an immigrant train as far as South Pass in Nebraska Territory, where the travelers had picked up another guide who would take them and their wagons on through the Rockies and over the Continental Divide. Fargo might have stayed with the wagon train the entire way, if a sudden fever had not claimed the lives of an entire family he had befriended. That cluster of lonely graves on the windswept prairie had reminded him too much of bitter losses in his own past, so when the train reached the trading post at South Pass, and he knew the pilgrims were in the capable hands of another guide, Fargo had turned and ridden away, heading east and keeping the mountains behind him.

By now the memories had receded, so he was looking forward with keen anticipation to spending some time in Omaha. As a rule, Fargo was not that fond of cities, but they came in mighty handy every so often, when a fella wanted to blow off some steam.

A few minutes later, Fargo tensed as the stallion slowed down and lifted its head, pricking up its ears. He was letting the Ovaro set the pace, as he usually did when there was no pressing need for speed. The horse's behavior told Fargo that it had seen or heard or smelled something out of the ordinary, or maybe a combination of all three things. Now that he had been alerted, he noticed that there was a distinct smell in the air, as if a cloud of dust had blown through here a short time earlier, and a faint haze lingered in the atmosphere.

That meant a large group of riders, Fargo thought. Out here on the plains, such a thing might be innocent . . . but the chances were greater that it boded ill for somebody.

The Ovaro did not stop, and Fargo did not rein in. He kept riding, seemingly unconcerned by anything around him, but his right hand went to the butt of the Colt on his hip and loosened the gun in its holster. His eyes flicked from side to side.

The stallion whinnied. With no more warning than that, a group of riders burst into view, urging their mounts up out of a wash to Fargo's right. He reined in sharply, pulling the big horse around in a half turn. His hand palmed out the Colt and started to lift it.

He stopped the gesture, not because he found himself facing the muzzles of half a dozen rifles but because he recognized the uniforms worn by the horsemen who were confronting him. The campaign caps and blue tunics and darker blue trousers with yellow stripes down the legs identified them as members of the United States Cavalry.

The men were all carrying .54 caliber carbines, which at the moment they had leveled at Fargo. "Hold it!" a strident voice shouted, and two more men rode out from behind the group of cavalrymen. One was a burly sergeant. The other bore the insignia of a lieutenant on his uniform. His face was young and untanned, Fargo noted, and that came as no surprise. There were plenty of shavetail lieutenants out here on the frontier. The Army had a bad habit of sending its young, inexperienced officers West for some seasoning. All too often, instead of making wily veterans out of them as the brass intended, the frontier just made those shavetails dead.

"Mister, I'll give you three seconds to holster that gun!" the lieutenant yelled at Fargo. He started to count. "One! . . ."

With a wry quirk of his mouth, Fargo slid the heavy revolver back into its holster. He wasn't going to give this youngster an excuse to get trigger-happy. He didn't much care for his high-handed attitude, though.

"Don't get a burr under your saddle, Lieutenant," Fargo said, his deep, calm voice carrying over the prairie without the need for shouting. "I'm not looking for trouble."

The young officer spurred his horse closer. The sergeant stayed close by his side. Tall, with broad, heavy shoulders, the noncom looked like he had all the experience and seasoning that the lieutenant lacked.

The lieutenant reined in, facing Fargo from a distance of ten feet. "What are you doing out here, mister?" he demanded.

Fargo sat easy in the saddle, his hands now crossed

and resting on the horn. "Didn't know the prairie was off-limits," he drawled, a faint, mocking smile on his lips.

"Just answer the lieutenant's question," the sergeant snapped. Fargo couldn't see any hair under the man's campaign cap. He appeared to be bald, despite being only in his thirties.

Fargo didn't like being bullied, and that seemed to be what these soldiers had in mind. But arguing with them would be just a waste of time, and besides, he tried to cooperate with the authorities, both military and civilian, whenever he could. "I'm bound for Omaha," he said. "Just looking to take it easy for a while and stock up on supplies while I'm there."

"Where are you coming from, and what were you doing there?" the lieutenant asked.

Fargo thought that the officer could have stood a lesson in frontier etiquette. It wasn't considered polite to ask a fella too many questions, especially when they concerned where he had been and what he was doing there. But again, Fargo wasn't looking to borrow trouble, so he said, "I've been over in Nebraska Territory, guiding a wagon train to South Pass."

"Do you have any proof of that?"

The lieutenant's persistent suspicion was starting to raise Fargo's hackles a little. "I've still got some of the money those immigrants paid me," he said, "but one gold piece looks pretty much like another, I reckon."

"Watch that smart mouth, mister," the sergeant said as he glowered at Fargo.

"I can handle this, Sergeant Creed," the lieutenant snapped with a sidewise glare at the noncom. Fargo took note of that, too, as well as the narrow-eyed look that the sergeant gave his superior officer. There was no love lost between these two.

The lieutenant turned his attention back to Fargo and asked, "What's your name?"

That was about enough, Fargo decided. He said, "Why don't you tell me what this is all about, Lieutenant? Do you have a reason for all these questions—or do you just not have enough to do today?"

The lieutenant's mouth drew down into a thin, angry line. Fargo expected an angry outburst, but after a moment, the young man said, "I'm Lieutenant Jackson Ross, in command of this detail from Headquarters Company, Department of the Platte, in Omaha. We're searching for the men responsible for a crime."

"What sort of crime?"

"That's none of your concern."

"I think it is," Fargo said, "when a few minutes ago it sounded like you were practically accusing me of being mixed up in it."

With a visible effort, Lieutenant Ross controlled his temper and impatience. "Two days ago, a United States Army supply train was on its way through this area. It was attacked, and the supplies being carried on the wagons were stolen."

"What kind of supplies?"

"That really *is* none of your business," Ross said.

Fargo leaned forward a little in the saddle. "Let me think about this," he said. "Somebody jumps a bunch of army supply wagons and makes off with what they're carrying. I don't reckon anybody would go to that much trouble for some barrels of salt pork and beans. Sounds more like what they took must have been guns."

Sergeant Creed said, "If you're such a smart son of a bitch, maybe you can tell us where those rifles are now."

Lieutenant Ross shot him an angry glance, then said to Fargo, "It was a shipment of new rifles bound for Fort Laramie, if you must know. What can you tell us about the raid?"

Fargo shook his head. "Not a damned thing. Two days ago I was a long way west of here. I haven't seen anybody suspicious between then and now, either. In fact, I haven't seen much of anybody. These plains are pretty empty between wagon trains."

"Why should we believe you?"

"Because I'm not in the habit of lying," Fargo said, his own irritation rising to the point where he was having trouble containing it.

"You'll pardon me, I'm sure, if I don't take your statements at face value."

Fargo said, "And you'll pardon me if I don't give a damn what you take and what you don't." He lifted the Ovaro's reins, preparing to ride around the cavalrymen. "Now, I'm going on my way."

Ross edged his horse over to block Fargo's path, and his hand moved to the snapped-down flap of the holster where he carried his sidearm. Creed said to him in a low, urgent voice, "Lieutenant, that fella can get his gun out and put four or five slugs through you by the time you unsnap that flap and haul out that pistol. Better take it easy."

Ross looked furious, but he took Creed's advice. He said contemptuously, "What would you have me do, then, Sergeant?"

"Leave this no-account drifter to me," Creed said, giving Fargo an ugly grin. "I'll beat the truth out of him."

Ross frowned. "I won't have you brawling with a civilian, Sergeant."

"What would you rather do with him? Have those troopers shoot him because he won't answer your questions?"

Ross hesitated before answering, torn by the situation in which his arrogance had placed him. Fargo could tell what the young officer was thinking. Ross didn't like the way Fargo had defied him, but it was an offense that hardly justified having the rest of the patrol open fire on him.

Coming to a decision, Ross said, "Very well, Sergeant. I'll leave the interrogation of this man to you."

That ugly grin stretched even farther across Creed's face. "Thanks, Lieutenant. I won't let you down." He looked at Fargo. "All right, mister. Now it's just you and me."

JUDSON GRAY

RANSOM RIDERS   20418-2

When Penn and McCutcheon are ambushed on their way to rescue a millionaire's kidnapped niece, they start to fear that the kidnapping was an inside job.

DOWN TO MARROWBONE   20158-2

Jim McCutcheon had squandered his Southern family's fortune and had to find a way to rebuild it among the boomtowns.

Jake Penn had escaped the bonds of slavery and had to find his long-lost sister...

Together, they're an unlikely team—but with danger down every trail, nothing's worth more than a friend you can count on...

JASON MANNING